"HE LOOKS DEAD," BILL SAID.

"Shut up!" Palmer snapped.

"Where's the money?" Dick asked. "He had a bag in his hands."

"He didn't have it," Palmer said. "He couldn't hold on to it once he got shot."

"Yer a liar!" Bill shouted. "Where'd you put it?" He looked at his brother. "They had time to stash it."

"Yeah, they did," Dick said, slowly, "but I don't think they woulda done that."

"I'm gonna look around," Bill said, not as trusting as his big brother.

"Go ahead," Palmer said, kneeling down next to Stan. "Can you hear me, Stan?"

"I hear everybody," Stan said. "I ain't dead yet." He opened his eyes, looked up at Dick. "You boys talked, didn'tcha?"

"What?" Dick said.

"Probably Billy, not you, Dick," Stan said.

"He didn't mean nothin', Stan," Dick said. "We're sorry you got shot."

"Tommy's right," Stan said. "You both left me there to die."

"Stan—"

Stan's bloody hand came up, holding his gun. He pointed it at Dick Evans and fired.

RALPH COMPTON

◊

THE WRONG SIDE OF THE LAW

A Ralph Compton Western by

ROBERT J. RANDISI

BERKLEY
New York

BERKLEY
An imprint of Penguin Random House LLC
penguinrandomhouse.com

Copyright © 2021 by The Estate of Ralph Compton
Penguin Random House supports copyright. Copyright fuels creativity, encourages
diverse voices, promotes free speech, and creates a vibrant culture. Thank you for buying
an authorized edition of this book and for complying with copyright laws by not
reproducing, scanning, or distributing any part of it in any form without permission.
You are supporting writers and allowing Penguin Random House to continue to
publish books for every reader.

BERKLEY and the BERKLEY & B colophon are registered trademarks of
Penguin Random House LLC.

ISBN: 9780593333853

First Edition: June 2021

Printed in the United States of America
1   3   5   7   9   10   8   6   4   2

Book design by George Towne

This is a work of fiction. Names, characters, places, and incidents either are the product
of the author's imagination or are used fictitiously, and any resemblance to actual persons,
living or dead, business establishments, events, or locales is entirely coincidental.

THE IMMORTAL COWBOY

This is respectfully dedicated to the "American Cowboy." His was the saga sparked by the turmoil that followed the Civil War, and the passing of more than a century has by no means diminished the flame.

———◦◦◦———

True, the old days and the old ways are but treasured memories, and the old trails have grown dim with the ravages of time, but the spirit of the cowboy lives on.

———◦◦◦———

In my travels—to Texas, Oklahoma, Kansas, Nebraska, Colorado, Wyoming, New Mexico, and Arizona—I always find something that reminds me of the Old West. While I am walking these plains and mountains for the first time, there is this feeling that a part of me is eternal, that I have known these old trails before. I believe it is the undying spirit of the frontier calling me, through the mind's eye, to step back into time. What is the appeal of the Old West of the American frontier?

———◦◦◦———

It has been epitomized by some as the dark and bloody period in American history. Its heroes—Crockett, Bowie, Hickok, Earp—have been reviled and criticized. Yet the Old West lives on, larger than life.

———◦◦◦———

It has become a symbol of freedom, when there was always another mountain to climb and another river to cross; when a dispute between two men was settled not with expensive lawyers, but with fists, knives, or guns. Barbaric? Maybe. But some things never change. When the cowboy rode into the pages of American history, he left behind a legacy that lives within the hearts of us all.

—*Ralph Compton*

CHAPTER ONE

TOM PALMER STUDIED the front of the bank from across the street. He'd been recruited for this job by his old friend Stan Hargrove, but he didn't like the rest of the men Stan had working with him. He wished he could talk Stan out of the job, but the older man was intent on hitting this bank in the town of Blackstone, New Mexico.

The town was growing, Stan had told him, and the bank was going to have the payrolls of several new businesses that were opening up, as well as those of a couple of big ranches in the area. "If there was ever a time to hit this bank, Tommy, it's now!" Stan said with enthusiasm.

Stan Hargrove was almost sixty, and he had spent the better part of his life as a small-time crook. He seemed to think that taking this bank was going to make him a big-time operator. So Tom had agreed to hold the horses while the old man went into the bank with Dick and Bill Evans.

But Palmer could see how the Evans brothers—who fancied themselves the James boys—snickered at Stan behind his back. It was only the year before, in North-field, Minnesota, that things had gone wrong for the James/Younger Gang. The Evans boys seemed to have forgotten that.

Palmer had been involved in many heists through-out the Southwest, whether they be banks or trains or stagecoaches, but up to this point, he had never killed anybody. He didn't want anyone killed during this job, either, especially not Stan Hargrove.

The Evans boys came walking toward the bank from one side, and Stan from the other. Palmer was to remain where he was and keep watch. He was also standing by the horses, which were across the street from the bank rather than right out front. A bunch of horses in front of a bank, that was a dead giveaway.

Stan went into the bank first, as planned. He was followed by the Evans boys, also according to plan. But when the shooting started, that was definitely not according to plan.

Palmer started to run across to the bank, but the doors opened and the two Evans boys came running out. They headed for the horses, trying to brush past Palmer, who reached out and grabbed Dick's arm.

"Where's Stan?"

"I dunno!" Dick Evans pulled his arm free and started running again.

Palmer headed for the bank again, saw Stan stagger through the door, holding one hand to his belly, which was blossoming red.

"Come on, Stan!" Palmer shouted, grabbing his friend's arm.

Some men with badges came out of the bank next with guns in their hands. Palmer half-dragged, half-carried Stan to the horses. The Evans boys had already mounted up and started riding away. That attracted the attention of the lawmen, who started shooting at them. This gave Palmer a chance to hoist Stan up onto his horse and to mount his own. Instead of lighting out in the same direction as the brothers, Palmer decided to go the opposite way, hoping it would take the lawmen valuable moments to realize what he was doing.

It was the precious time Palmer and Hargrove needed to get out of town. . . .

THE ORIGINAL PLAN, if the men got separated, was to meet a few miles out of town, in a clearing they had scouted days before. Palmer had no way of knowing if the Evans boys would be there, or if they had any money from the bank job, but he headed for the meeting place, just the same.

He managed to get to the clearing and keep Stan mounted until they got there. He leaped from his horse in time to catch the older man as he finally fell off. He lowered his friend to the ground easily, got him onto his back.

"Let me see," he said, trying to move Stan's hands from his midsection.

"It's bad, Tommy," Stan said. "Real bad."

"What happened, Stan?"

"It was those Evans boys," Stan said. "They spent the night drinking at a whorehouse."

"And they opened their big mouths?" Palmer said. "I warned you about them, Stan. I told you—"

"Yeah, yeah," Stan said, "can we save the I-told-ya-sos for another time? Maybe at my grave?"

"Stan—"

"I just wanna live long enough to hear what them boys got to say," Stan went on.

"If they have the nerve to show up here," Palmer said.

"They will," Stan said.

"How do you know?"

"They don't know if I got away with the money or not," Stan said. "I had it in my hands, Tommy. I had it! But then them lawmen started shootin'."

Palmer went to his horse for his canteen, held Stan's head while the man drank, then removed his bandanna and poured some water on it.

"Let me clean your wound and get a look, Stan."

"Ahhhh, go ahead," Stan finally said. He dropped his hand away from his belly, and blood just seemed to spurt out. As he had said, it was bad. Palmer couldn't clean it, so he simply tried to stanch the flow of blood with the bandanna.

"Owww, watch it!" Stan snapped, his face etched with pain.

"Sorry, Stan."

At that point they both heard horses approaching.

"A posse?" Stan asked. "Or Dick and Bill?"

Palmer stood up to have a look. If it was a posse, he didn't intend to leave Stan alone, but he doubted the town could have put one together that fast. Then he saw there were only two riders.

"It's the Evans boys," he said. He remained standing and waited.

The two riders reined in their horses and dismounted. Before they could speak, Palmer hit Dick Evans in the mouth with his fist, knocking the older brother on his ass.

"What the hell—" Bill snapped, his hand moving toward his gun.

"Easy, Billy," Dick said, getting to his feet. "Tommy's just a little pissed about Stan gettin' shot."

"You left him there!" Palmer shouted. "The two of you lit out and left him behind. I had to get him and drag him to his horse."

"Then he's lucky he had you," Dick said, wiping blood from his mouth with the back of his hand. "How is he?"

"Not good," Palmer said.

They all looked down at the supine man, whose eyes were now closed, his face ashen.

"He looks dead," Bill said.

"Shut up!" Palmer snapped.

"Where's the money?" Dick asked. "He had a bag in his hands."

"He didn't have it," Palmer said. "He couldn't hold on to it once he got shot."

"Yer a liar!" Bill shouted. "Where'd you put it?" He looked at his brother. "They had time to stash it."

"Yeah, they did," Dick said, slowly, "but I don't think they woulda done that."

"I'm gonna look around," Bill said, not as trusting as his big brother.

"Go ahead," Palmer said, kneeling down next to Stan. "Can you hear me, Stan?"

"I hear everybody," Stan said. "I ain't dead yet." He opened his eyes, looked up at Dick. "You boys talked, didn'tcha?"

"What?" Dick said.

"Probably Billy, not you, Dick," Stan said. "Bragged to some whore, didn't he?"

"He didn't mean nothin', Stan," Dick said. "We're sorry you got shot."

"Tommy's right," Stan said. "You both left me there to die."

"Stan—"

Stan's bloody hand came up, holding his gun. He pointed it at Dick Evans and fired.

"Wha—" Billy said, startled. He turned from searching Stan's saddlebag, reached for his gun. Palmer had no choice but to draw his own gun and fire. The bullet struck Billy just below the chin, snapping his head back. He was dead before he hit the ground.

Palmer turned to look at Dick Evans, who was on his back, staring at the sky. It was just at that moment Palmer saw the light go out in his eyes. Both Evans brothers were dead. Tom Palmer couldn't really blame Stan Hargrove for what he had done. Things had gone horribly wrong, and they hadn't had to.

"Stan, let's get you—" he said, looking over at his friend, but it was clear at that moment that Palmer was the only one left alive.

THE PREVIOUS NIGHT the four of them had sat together in the Straight Flush Saloon, going over last-minute plans for the bank job.

"And don't anybody get drunk and talk to no whores" was the last thing Stan said.

"Ya think we're stupid or somethin', old man?" Bill demanded.

"I think *you* are, yeah," Stan said. "Dick, you gotta control your brother."

"Old-timer," Bill said angrily, "you gotta control yer mouth!"

Well, as it turned out, Stan's mouth had been right on the money.

Palmer wasn't going to leave that clearing without giving his friend a decent burial. And he did the decent thing and buried the brothers, too—although they had to share the same shallow, unmarked grave.

Once he was done, he went through the brothers' saddlebags for whatever supplies he could salvage—and, truth be told, to make sure that neither one of them was holding out and had the money. He got some coffee, a pot, some beef jerky, a bag of makings, but not a dime between them. He didn't have the heart to take anything from his friend, so he simply tossed Stan's saddlebags into the grave with him. He unsaddled all three horses and set them free and dug a fourth hole for the saddles. If a posse came this way, he didn't want them to find anything helpful.

The job going bad and losing Stan had convinced Palmer that it was time for a change in his life. And for that to happen, he had to have a clean slate. While digging, he made up his mind to ride north. He knew there were plenty of wanted posters on him floating around the Southwest. First chance he got, he'd have to shave off his beard to change his appearance. He hated to do it, because he'd had the facial hair for ten years, but it was time to go clean-shaven. He didn't think there were any posters on him looking clean-shaven.

He stood over his friend's grave and felt bad that he

couldn't put a marker on it. He also felt bad that, not being a religious man, he had no idea what final words to say. So he just said, "So long, Stan."

After he'd done everything he could to cover his trail, he mounted his pony and rode north.

CHAPTER TWO

I T WAS THE smoke that drew Palmer to the site of the burned wagon. The flames had long since died down, but the smoke was still drifting straight up, as if from a chimney.

He topped a rise and looked across the Great Plains of South Dakota Territory. He spotted the wreckage of not one wagon, but two. He looked around, didn't see anyone in any direction. Since he'd been forced to leave his last town in a hurry, his pockets were mostly empty, as was his canteen. He wasn't normally the kind of person to pick through the bones of the dead, but in this instance he didn't seem to have any other choice. The wagons were there, nobody else was around, and he was in need.

He urged his tired pony on and rode toward the smoking remains. As he approached, a scent other than that of burning wood came to his nostrils—

torched flesh. He wasn't looking forward to what he was going to find, but he kept riding.

As he got closer, the pony began to shy away from the combined smells, and Palmer had to urge him on. Finally, he took pity on the horse and stopped far enough away from the scene for the animal to relax. He dismounted and walked to the burned remnants of two Conestoga wagons.

Palmer's talents lay in bank, stage, and train robberies. He wasn't a tracker and didn't read sign, but he could see that the tracks in the dirt around the wagons were from unshod horses—likely Indian ponies. He knew that several Sioux tribes called this area home and probably didn't like having wagons carrying whites crossing their land. And he knew that the Sioux, even if they had waited and gone picking through the rubble, would have left some things behind that were of no value to them, but were valuable to Palmer.

He saw the bodies and winced. There were a man, a woman, and three children. He knew there could have been more kids, for the Indians would probably have carried away any who had survived the attack. They liked taking young boys to raise as slaves and young girls as wives. These children appeared to be two teenage girls and a small boy who had taken an arrow in the back—which may have simply been accidental. The adults seemed to have been in their late thirties, which was roughly his age, and each had several arrows piercing their bodies. Palmer was pleased to see that none of the dead had been scalped. Scalping was actually a practice instituted by whites so they could collect bounties on the Indians they killed. There were savages on both sides, red and white.

There were no horses around. The Indians would definitely have taken them. Palmer also didn't see any blankets or much in the way of clothing. Those were also things that would have been taken. There were no guns.

Although it went against the grain for him to go through a dead man's pockets, he forced himself and came away with some paper money and coins, both of which the Indians would've left. It came to about forty dollars, which almost made him feel rich—guilty, but rich.

In the back of one of the burned-out wagons, he found an open trunk. Some articles of clothing had been removed and tossed about; others must have been taken away. He knew Indians liked colorful clothing, especially women's dresses. They took them for their squaws and sometimes even wore the dresses themselves. The other thing he couldn't find neither hide nor hair of was whiskey. If there had been any, the Indians would've gotten it. He did find a barrel that was still half filled with water, and so dipped his canteen in to fill it.

He was almost satisfied with what he had gotten and ready to leave these folks in peace when he saw some papers blowing in the slight breeze. He gathered them up, smoothed them out, and read a few of them. Most were letters, but not from family members or friends. A few were from the mayor and town council of a town called Integrity. The dead man was apparently on his way there to become the town's new marshal. According to the letters, the officials of Integrity were very impressed with his history as a lawman back East, and were very pleased that he was looking to do the same work as he came west with his family. The last letter was the formal offer of the job, complete with a house for him and his family to live in.

Palmer carried the correspondence back to his horse and stuffed it in one of his saddlebags. There was a thought brewing in his brain, but he needed time to allow it to take root. He decided these folks deserved a decent burial, and he could roll the idea over in his head while digging.

B Y THE TIME he had dug the five graves—rather than one mass grave, which had been his first idea—Palmer had decided what to do. He was wanted for several different crimes in some of the Southwest territories, which was the actual reason he had ridden north in the first place. But he had left Colorado rather quickly, hadn't felt safe enough to stop in Wyoming or Montana, but had run out of funds and now needed a place to stop. And when he got there, he was going to need a job.

What had befallen this family was a tragedy, but it put a job right in his lap. Abraham Cassidy had been on his way to take the job as town marshal of Integrity, South Dakota. From the letters Palmer had read, nobody in that town had ever met the man in person. They were hiring him based on an exchange of information in the mail. All Palmer had to do was show up in Integrity with those letters, and the job would be his. And what would be so hard about working as a lawman? He'd spent enough time in the company of them over the years to be able to impersonate one—

just for a while, until he figured out what his next move should be.

In the letters the town fathers told Cassidy the town was a small, quiet place. If Palmer had to jail a few drunks on Saturday night and shoot a stray dog or two, he could certainly do it.

There was nothing he could do about the burned-out remnants of the wagons. After he finished burying the family, he mounted up and headed north for Integrity.

W HEN HE CAMPED that night, he took care of his beard, first chopping it away with his knife, then shaving it off. He'd found a small amount of coffee in one of the burned-out wagons and still had a piece of beef jerky, so he made a meal out of that.

He thought about starting the next day living as Abraham Cassidy, lawman, family man, good man. Could he do all that? Especially the good-man part? He didn't know for certain, but he sure as hell was going to give it a try. At least for a while. He needed to let things cool off down south, let all the wanted posters on him fall down to the bottom of the pile.

In the morning he rose, put his hand to his face, and remembered.

He was a new man. . . .

P ALMER REALIZED HE was going to have to tell a story when he reached Integrity. After all, where was his wife and where were his children? Why was he riding a horse rather than driving his wagons? And he had been wearing the same clothes for weeks now. He'd had a shave, but he was going to need a bath and some new clothes.

Since "Abraham Cassidy" was coming from the East, were the people of Integrity going to expect him to arrive all duded up? They must have known he was traveling with wagons and all his belongings, but when Palmer buried the man, he noticed his clothes had been Western garb, not Eastern duds. Apparently, the man had already started to dress for his new job.

Palmer's only problem was going to be talking about the East. He'd never been that way, and Cassidy was a man who had lived there, probably all his life. Palmer was going to have to come up with a story for why he didn't want to talk about it. He could claim it was too painful a subject, what with his wife and children having been killed by Indians.

He was also going to have to do something about the way he spoke. He'd had some education when he was younger, and by the time he ran away from home at sixteen, he hadn't spoken like his farmer parents. Now he thought he sounded like an educated man, but he might have to ramp that up some as Marshal Abraham Cassidy. So while he rode, he practiced saying some words a little differently, not shortening them or dropping his "g"s so much.

He didn't know how much farther Integrity was, so when he came to a town called Birchmont, he stopped to buy some clean clothes and a new hat. He needed to arrive in Integrity looking newly dressed for the West.

Birchmont had a small mercantile store, where Palmer used a portion of his forty dollars to outfit himself. After that, he found a small café and had his first hot meal in some time, a steaming bowl of beef stew.

"Wow," the motherly waitress commented, "you look like you ain't eaten in weeks."

"Not that long," Palmer said, speaking slowly, "but it's been a while."

"I think I can get ya some extra, if you like," she told him.

"That'd be great, ma'am," he said. "I'd be much oblig—very grateful."

She smiled and took his bowl, saying, "I like to see a man with a hearty appetite. Besides, ain't much business today, so I might as well empty the pot for ya."

He looked around at all the empty tables as she went to the kitchen. It seemed he had come in at just the right time to get the most for his money. Maybe his luck was changing, after all. . . .

HE LEFT BIRCHMONT with new clothes and a full stomach. He wondered about buying a new horse, but decided against it. His pony would be exhausted by the time they got to Integrity, but he'd be able to explain that with no trouble.

Nobody in Birchmont knew how far it was to Integrity, but in the next town—Dexterville—a man told him he still had about a day's ride.

"You're gonna come to a crossroads," the man told him. "North will be Deadwood, and east, Integrity."

"Much oblig— Thank you," Palmer said.

"That pony looks plumb tuckered out," the man said.

"That makes two of us," Palmer said, "but I'm sure we'll make it. Thanks again."

* * *

H E CAME TO the crossroads, as the man had pre-
dicted. Under normal circumstances he might
have headed for the town he had heard of, Deadwood,
where Wild Bill Hickok had been killed. In fact he
paused there, considering it. If he went to Integrity, he
was committing himself to becoming "Marshal Abraham Cassidy." How long would he be able to keep that
guise up? Not only a lawman, but a widower who had
lost his children. He saw only two ways he could be
found out. One, if somebody dug those bodies up and
found the real Cassidy. And two, if someone rode into
Integrity and recognized him for who he truly was. He
felt fairly sure that anyone coming to this crossroads
would head for Deadwood. What were the chances
somebody he knew, or who knew him, would come riding into Integrity? And even if they did, would they
recognize him without his beard?

He turned the pony's head east and kept riding.

W HEN PALMER RODE into Integrity he saw that the
description in the letters of a "small town" was
a slight overstatement. He had been in plenty of towns
smaller than this one.

He rode down the main street—which he noticed was
labeled Front Street—past a couple of saloons and hotels. Farther down were a mercantile store, a hardware
store, a barbershop, a leather goods store, a small café,
and what looked like a brand-new marshal's office.

He didn't know if he should stop and get a room at
one of the hotels, find a livery stable, or go to the mar-

shal's office or a saloon, but then he spotted another new building. Over the doorway it said **CITY HALL**. That seemed the likeliest place to find out where he should go. He reined in his pony in front, dismounted, and tied the animal off, although he thought it was probably too tired to wander off.

He tried the double doors to the city hall, found them unlocked, and entered. He stood in an open hall with a stairway just ahead of him. He looked around, then saw what appeared to be a directory on the wall next to the door. When he took a look, he saw a list of offices, which included the OFFICE OF THE MAYOR, the TOWN COUNCIL, something called a CITY PLANNER. There was another entitled COUNTY DEEDS, and still another that said TREASURER.

Palmer had folded some of the letters and put them in his pocket. He took them out now and noticed that many of them had been signed: *Office of the Mayor*, with the mayor's name below that: *Victor O'Connor*.

The decision made, he looked at the directory, saw that the office of the mayor was on the second floor, in room 201. He proceeded up the stairs, found room 201, tried the door, realized that it was unlocked, and entered. A middle-aged woman seated at a desk looked up at him from behind her wire-framed glasses and smiled.

"Welcome to the mayor's office," she said. "Can I help you? Do you have an appointment to see His Honor?"

"I guess I do," Palmer said, and then announced out loud for the first time, "I'm Abraham Cassidy."

"Oh!" she said, looking delighted. "You're our new marshal."

"That I am, ma'am," Palmer said. "That I am."

She stood up quickly and said, "Oh, let me tell His Honor that you're here."

And as she hustled away to deliver the news, Palmer was truly committed.

CHAPTER THREE

MAYOR VICTOR O'CONNOR had been in office for two years. One of his first jobs had been to find a lawman for Integrity. He decided to look a little farther than the West. He didn't want just another lawman, one who had worn the badge in many different towns and territories. He wanted a lawman who was as new to the job as he was. That way they could bond over making Integrity the kind of town it should be.

When his assistant, Mrs. McQueen, came in and announced that their new marshal had arrived, his normally dour face lit up.

"Well, send him in, Mrs. McQueen," he said. "Send him in. Let's not keep our new lawman waiting."

"Yes, Your Honor."

She turned and went back out. Seconds later the door opened and Marshal Abraham Cassidy walked in.

* * *

WHEN PALMER ENTERED the office, he expected to find a stodgy old politician in a dark suit. Instead the man seated behind the desk was a sad-looking fellow who looked like he hadn't yet turned forty.

"Mr. Cassidy?" the man said. "Or should I say, Marshal Cassidy."

"Mr. Mayor?" Palmer said.

The two men met in the center of the room and shook hands heartily.

"Mayor Victor O'Connor, at your service," the mayor said. "Do you mind if I ask for some kind of . . ."

"Proof?" Palmer finished. He took the letters from his pocket. "Like these?"

The mayor took the letters, looked at them, smiled, and handed them back.

"Good enough," he said. "And your family? Are they waiting outside?"

Palmer adopted as sad a look as he could.

"I'm afraid my family was killed by Indians," he said. "I fought them as well as I could, but . . ."

"That's terrible!"

"What's terrible is the fact that I'm the only one who managed to survive," Palmer said. "When it was over, the only thing I could think to do was bury them and then come here and do what I came west to do."

"Yes, of course," the mayor said. "So you're still going to take the job?"

"If I don't," Palmer said, "then my family died for no reason, and I'll have . . . nothing."

"I suppose that's the only . . . sane way to think about it," the mayor said.

He turned, walked quickly to his desk, opened the top drawer, took something out, and brought it back to Palmer.

"This is yours," he said.

Palmer accepted the marshal's badge from the man, stared at it as it lay in the palm of his hand.

"Do you want to . . . pin it on?" Mayor O'Connor asked.

"Not at the moment," Palmer said. "If you don't mind, I'll take today to get used to the idea and start in on the job tomorrow."

"Of course, of course," the mayor said. "Meanwhile I can show you the office and your, uh, house."

"Um, yes, the house," Palmer said. "Without my family, I don't think I'll be needing a house, Mr. Mayor. A hotel room would probably suit me better."

"Of course," O'Connor said. "I'll make those arrangements quickly so you can get settled. Why don't we walk over to the hotel together?"

The mayor got his jacket and hat, and they left the office together.

"Is that your horse?" the mayor asked when they got to the street.

"It is."

"He looks worn out," O'Connor said. "When we get to the hotel, I'll have somebody take it to the livery stable for you."

"I appreciate that."

Palmer untied his horse and led it as he and the mayor walked to the hotel.

"I'll get you a room in the Utopia Hotel. It's the best in town."

"I really don't need the best," Palmer said. "Just a bed and a dining room would be nice."

"We'll start with the Utopia and see what happens," the mayor said.

When they reached the hotel, Palmer once again tied his horse off, then looked up at the two-story structure, which appeared to be new.

"It's only been open about two months," O'Connor said, confirming that fact. "Brand-new."

"That's great," Palmer said, and they went inside.

"Afternoon, Mr. Mayor," the well-dressed clerk said. He was in his thirties, wearing a dark suit and tie, with his hair parted in the middle and slicked down.

"Edgar, this is our new marshal, Abraham Cassidy."

"Just Abe," Palmer said.

"Abe needs a room," the mayor said.

The clerk looked confused.

"I thought we were giving the new marshal and his family a house," he said.

"Just give him a room, Edgar," O'Connor said. "It'll all be explained."

"Whatever you say, Mayor," Edgar said. "We're happy to have you, Marshal." He turned, took a key off the wall behind him, and handed it to Palmer, saying, "I'll give you room seven. It's a two-room suite."

"Much oblig— Uh, thank you," Palmer said.

"Edgar, have somebody take the marshal's horse to the livery stable," the mayor said, "and bring his saddlebags up to the room."

"No luggage?" Edgar asked.

"That will also be explained," the mayor said. "Shall I walk you up, Marshal?"

"I can find it, Mayor," Palmer said.

"Good, good," O'Connor said. "Why don't you get freshened up and meet me down here in the lobby in an hour? You must be hungry. We'll have an early supper and then I'll show you your office."

"Sounds good," Palmer said. "I'll see you then."

As Palmer went to the stairs and started up, he looked back and saw the mayor talking to the clerk in low tones, probably explaining about the marshal's dead "family."

Palmer got to room seven and let himself in. Compared to most of the hotels Palmer had been hiding out in the past few months, it was lavish. There were a colorful sofa, a matching armchair, a round wooden table surrounded by two chairs with a lamp on it. The next room had a large bed with a chest of drawers and a dresser with a mirror, a lamp on a small table by the bed, and one on the wall by the doorway. On top of the dresser were a pitcher and a basin. He removed his gun belt, set it down on the bed, took off his shirt, filled the basin with water from the pitcher, and proceeded to wash his face, neck, torso, arms, and hands. At some point over the next few days, he would have a real bath. Followed by a visit to the barber. By the time that was all done, he wouldn't resemble the face on any wanted poster that might show up.

There was a knock on the door and a bellboy smiled as he opened the door and said, "Here're your saddle-bags, Marshal."

"Thank you."

After he closed the door, he realized he had done so without tipping the youngster. If he was going to live there and expect good service, he was going to have to make up for that.

He had a fresh shirt in the saddlebags, which he had only recently bought. He took it out and put it on, looked at himself in the mirror while he buttoned it. He usually stayed away from anything bright, like red or yellow, not wanting to be noticed. This shirt was dark blue. But since he was the law here, there was really no need for him to try to go unnoticed. He wouldn't be wearing a shirt for as long as he had on the trail, so maybe he would buy a few of different colors. He was going to have to come up with a personality for "Marshal Abe Cassidy" that didn't match his own.

He hadn't bought himself new Levi's or found a new hat he liked, so his old clothes needed to be pounded a bit to get the trail dust off. He decided not to do it in the room, though. He opened his door, stepped out into the empty hallway, and used his hat to slap as much of the dust off him as he could, then hurriedly stepped back inside before anyone saw him.

There was a window in the front room, but none in the bedroom. He walked to the window and looked out, found himself staring down at Front Street. There was no access to his room from outside the window, which suited him. He always preferred to have rooms that were not reachable from a balcony.

He had noticed in the lobby that there was a doorway leading to the saloon next door, which he assumed went by the same name—Utopia. He decided to go down and have a beer before he met the mayor in the lobby.

He had placed the badge on the top of the dresser when he walked in. Now he walked to it and picked it up, considered pinning it on, but decided against it. Like he'd told the mayor, he'd wait for the next day to pin it on and start his job—his life.

He put the badge into his shirt pocket, strapped on his gun, and left the room.

CHAPTER FOUR

PALMER ENTERED THE saloon, stopped just inside to have a look. More than a saloon, it looked like a cattlemen's club, with green felt and leather all around. At that time of the afternoon, there were only a few customers, and Palmer was willing to bet they were all guests of the hotel.

He walked to the bar and was met there by a young bartender wearing a white shirt and a green vest.

"What are you supposed to be?" Palmer asked.

"Yeah, I know," the bartender said. "I feel stupid wearing this, but the manager insisted and I wanted this job. New guest?"

"That's right," Palmer said, "I just checked in an hour ago."

"One beer on the house comin' up, then," the barman said.

"I won't argue with that," Palmer said.

"Here ya go," the barman said, setting the beer down in front of his customer.

"What's your name?" Palmer asked as he picked it up.

"I'm Simon."

"Glad to meet you, Simon," Palmer said. "I'm Abe Cassidy." He took the badge from his pocket and showed it to the man. "Marshal Abe Cassidy."

"The new marshal!" Simon said as Palmer tucked the badge away again. "Why aren't you wearin' the tin?"

"I start the job tomorrow," Palmer said. "Today I'm just another customer."

"That suits me, Marshal," Simon said, leaning on the bar. "So are you gonna be livin' in the hotel?"

"For a while," Palmer said. "Until I find something... different."

"The word I heard was we were gettin' a family man as a marshal," Simon said.

"You were," Palmer said, "until the Sioux killed my wife and kids. Now it's just me."

"I'm sorry to hear that."

"Yeah." Palmer drained his beer and slapped the mug down. "I've got to meet the mayor for supper, but how about a whiskey first?"

"Comin' up!"

WHEN PALMER LEFT the saloon and entered the lobby, the mayor was already there, waiting.

"There you are, Marshal," he said as Palmer approached him.

"Now I'm ready to eat."

"I'll take you to the best place in town," O'Connor

said. "At this time of the day, it shouldn't be too hard to get a table." He grinned. "Especially if you're the mayor. Come on, we can walk."

The restaurant turned out to be three streets away from the Utopia Hotel. It was called the Stallion Steak House. As they entered, a man in a black suit approached them.

"Mr. Mayor, a little early tonight?"

"Jack, this is our new marshal, Abe Cassidy. I want you to give him a good meal."

"Of course, sir," Jack said. "Your regular table is waiting."

Jack walked them across the room to a table for two.

"Would you gents like to start with something to drink?" he asked.

"Marshal?" the mayor said.

"Just a cold beer."

"The same for me, Jack," O'Connor said.

"Yes, sir. Your waiter will be right over to take your order."

As Jack walked away, Palmer said, "It's been a while since I had a good steak."

"Then that's what you'll have," the mayor said. "You know, for a fella who's from the East, you wear that gun on your hip like you know how to use it."

"We had guns back East, Mr. Mayor," Palmer told him.

"Yes, of course," O'Connor said.

A short, bandy-legged man came over with their beers and to take their order. The mayor said, "Two steak dinners, Arthur."

"Comin' up, Mr. Mayor."

"So tell me about my new home, Mr. Mayor. Your letters made it sound like a much smaller town."

"It's a town on the rise, Marshal," O'Connor said. "Deadwood seems to be turning into a ghost town and it looks like we're taking up the slack. Hence the new hotel, new businesses like this one, and the new city hall."

"And the new marshal."

"Exactly."

"And is my office new?"

"I'm afraid not," O'Connor said. "It's our old sheriff's office, but it's been cleaned up."

"I'm sure it'll be fine," Palmer said.

"Hopefully," the mayor said, "you won't have much use for the jail cells, except maybe on Saturday nights."

"I'm with you there, Mr. Mayor," Palmer said.

"Ah, here come the steaks. . . ."

A FTER THEY FINISHED eating, Palmer thought he'd probably be taking many of his meals there, especially if they were part of the job. He didn't see the mayor pay a bill, so he wondered if the marshal would be receiving the same consideration.

They left the steak house, O'Connor saying, "All right, let's go and see your office."

The office was, indeed, an old sheriff's office. Palmer had been in many over the years, and this one was very familiar. There were a desk, a gun rack, a potbellied stove, and a wall peg to hang his hat and the cellblock keys on.

"I'm sure at some point the town council will be approving plans for a new marshal's office," Mayor O'Connor said.

"This is fine, Mr. Mayor," Palmer said. "All I'll need to add is a coffeepot."

"You grab whatever you think you need from the mercantile, and the town will foot the bill."

"It won't be much," Palmer said. "I wouldn't want to take advantage of that offer."

As they stepped back outside the mayor said, "Well, that's everything, unless you, ah, actually want to see the house we were going to give you and your family."

"That's not necessary," Palmer said.

"And what about your family?" O'Connor said. "Will you want some of us to go out with you and recover their bodies so they can be buried here?"

"That won't be necessary," Palmer said. "I'm not the type of man who would be spending a lot of time at grave sites. I mean, it's only their bodies, isn't it? They're not really there."

"I suppose not," O'Connor said. "I guess they're, uh, in your heart."

"Exactly."

"Of course," O'Connor went on, "we do have a priest and a parson, each with their own church. You might want to have a talk with one of them."

"I'm not exactly what you'd call a religious man, Mr. Mayor," Palmer said, "but you know, I might just do that."

They headed back to the Utopia Hotel.

"You can have your suite here as long as you want it, Marshal," O'Connor said in the lobby. "I'll make the arrangements with the owner."

"As long as I'm not taking advantage," Palmer said.

"As our lawman, you're going to be entitled to certain, uh, extras, and this will be one of them."

"I'm much obliged, Mr. Mayor," Palmer said. "I

think I might spend the rest of the evening just getting to know the town a little."

"My house is on the north end of town, Marshal," O'Connor said. "If you need anything, please don't hesitate to stop by."

"I'll stop by your office in the morning with the badge on, as I start my first day," Palmer said.

"Excellent!" O'Connor said. "I'll look forward to seeing you wearing it."

"Thanks for the steak," Palmer said.

O'Connor nodded, turned, and left the hotel. Palmer knew that politicians always had their own agenda. He figured he would find out what O'Connor's was sometime in the future. At that moment, the mayor was putting his best foot forward.

Palmer gave the mayor some time to put some distance between himself and the hotel, then stepped back outside and started to stroll. The badge was still in his pocket, so no one on the street gave him a second look. He was a stranger who got a glance or two, but that was it.

As he passed the mercantile, he saw that it was closed for the day, so he put the location in the back of his mind. In the morning he would stop in for his coffeepot and a few other essentials.

He passed both of the churches the mayor had referred to, but didn't go inside either. He truly wasn't a religious man, and the people he had buried were not actually Tom Palmer's family. Any sadness or regret he would show as "Marshal Abe Cassidy" would have to be contrived.

As he passed several of the saloons, they were coming to life for the evening, with lights, music, and noise. He decided to wait until he was actually wearing the badge to go inside one of the saloons.

Heading back to his hotel, he was wondering if he was doing the right thing. In point of fact, no, it definitely wasn't the right thing to do, but his question had to be, was it right for him? He was walking the other side of that thin line between right and wrong for the first time. He had no idea what it would be like to be a lawman, but working the right side of the law for a change was certainly going to be interesting.

When he reached his hotel he decided to go right to his room and not stop in the hotel saloon again. He was feeling weary from all the travel and decided it was just time to rest his bones.

CHAPTER FIVE

W**HEN PALMER WOKE** the next morning, it was as Marshal Abraham Cassidy. He washed his face, got dressed, but when it came to pinning on the badge, he still hesitated. There was one more thing he had to do.

He went down to the front desk to the smiling clerk.

"Can I help you, sir?"

"I need a bath—" Palmer started.

"I can arrange that—"

"And a haircut. Can you direct me to somewhere I can get both?"

"There is a barber two blocks from here who has bathtubs in his back rooms, but we can also offer you both right here."

"You have a barber who works for the hotel?"

"Yes," the clerk said, "which means he won't charge you for the haircut. And we will not charge you for the bath."

"All right, then," Palmer said. "I'll go upstairs and get some fresh clothes."

"I'll have everything ready for you when you come back down . . . Marshal."

"Much obliged."

He turned and went back upstairs.

A FTER HIS HAIRCUT and shave, Palmer walked down the hall to a room with a large wooden bathtub. He soaked in it a while, then got out, dried off, and put on his fresh shirt and vest. He still needed to buy some new trousers, but that could wait. The last thing he did before going to the hotel dining room for breakfast was pin on the marshal's badge.

A FTER BATHING AND eating breakfast, Palmer went to city hall to present himself, badge and all, to the mayor as Marshal Abe Cassidy.

"Marshal!" Mayor O'Connor said as Palmer entered the office. "Good morning."

"Good morning, Mr. Mayor," Palmer said. "I just wanted to let you know I'm on the job." He tapped the badge on his chest.

"That's good to hear," O'Connor said. "Can I offer you some coffee?"

"No, sir," Palmer said. "I'd better get to my office and see what I have to do to get it in order."

"Just one minute, Marshal," O'Connor said. "I'm arranging for a meeting here at city hall to present you to the town fathers."

"When would that be, Mr. Mayor?"

"Hopefully as soon as tomorrow night. I just want you to know so that you'll be there."

"You can count on me," Palmer said.

"Good, good," O'Connor said. "Then have a productive first day on the job, Marshal."

"Thank you."

Palmer left city hall and walked to his office.

A FTER MARSHAL CASSIDY left city hall, Mayor O'Connor came out of his office.

"Mrs. McQueen," he said, "please notify the town council members that I need them for a meeting tomorrow night at seven p.m."

"Yes, sir," she said. "May I tell them what it's about?"

"Yes," he said, "tell them they'll be welcoming our new marshal to town. And post a notice that the public is also welcome to attend."

It was short notice to get a public announcement posted around town, but Mrs. McQueen said, "Yes, sir, right away."

O'Connor went back into his office, knowing the woman would manage to get it done.

The next day would mark a new start for the town of Integrity.

P ALMER ENTERED THE marshal's office, stopped just inside the door, and looked around. He had a coffeepot and some coffee in his hands, as well as his rifle. He walked to the potbellied stove, looked inside, and saw that he was going to need some makings for a fire, so he set the coffee aside.

He walked to the gun rack on the wall. More of the spaces were empty than full, but there were a rifle and a shotgun that were in desperate need of some cleaning. He put his own rifle in one of the empty slots.

The desk was covered with a layer of dust. He looked around, found some rags and a broom, and proceeded to start cleaning the place up.

After a few hours, he was seated at his dust-free desk with a fresh cup of coffee. Also on the desk were the rifle and the shotgun that had been in the rack when he entered. He thought he might take them apart and clean them, make sure they were in working order. If they weren't, he'd get rid of them.

It took about an hour to dismantle the weapons, clean them properly, and reassemble them, and then he worked on his own rifles and pistol. He was finishing up when the door opened and a man walked in. He was in his late twenties, a tall, rangy man with a serious-looking face.

"You the new marshal?" he asked.

"I am," Palmer said. "Marshal Cassidy. What can I do for you?"

"I'm Steve Atlee," the man said.

"And?"

"I'm your deputy."

"I don't have a deputy," Palmer said.

"Well, I mean," Atlee said, "I could be your deputy. You're gonna need one, ya know?"

"I don't know," Palmer said. "Not really. I mean, I just started the job myself. I'll have to see if I have a need for deputies."

"Well, if you do, I'm your man," Atlee said.

"Do you have experience?"

"Not exactly," Atlee said. "I mean, I always volunteer when there's a posse."

"How many times have you ridden with one?"

"Well . . . none, but—"

"Mr. Atlee," Palmer said, "I'll let you know what I decide."

"Thanks, Marshal," Atlee said, and left.

Palmer had never thought about having deputies. He still wasn't sure he knew how to be a lawman himself, how could he tell others how to do it?

He walked to the window and looked out at the people passing by on the street. As of today, their welfare—maybe their lives—was in his hands. He touched the badge on his chest. Now that he'd pinned it on, there was no point in having negative thoughts. Even if he didn't uphold the law the way most lawmen did, he could find a way to do it himself. After all, he knew all sorts of ways to break it.

He decided to walk around town and let the people see him and the badge.

H ALF OF THE people he encountered ignored him; the others exchanged some sort of greeting—a nod, a tip of the hat. He finished his walk and made his first visit to a saloon. He chose one called the Palomino.

As he entered the busy saloon, about half the heads turned to have a curious look, then turned away. A few might have noticed the badge, but no one seemed to have an obvious adverse reaction to the law. More important, Palmer didn't recognize anyone, and nobody seemed to know him. He touched his upper lip, where he had left a mustache when he shaved his beard. Now that he was thinking about it, he should get rid of it, too. Present a whole new, fresh face to the world. Then maybe he wouldn't have to worry every time he walked into a crowded saloon.

He walked to the bar and found a spot with no trouble.

"The new marshal, right?" the middle-aged bartender asked without smiling. "What can I get ya, Marshal?"

"A beer, thanks."

"Sure."

"How much?" Palmer asked when the bartender put the mug in front of him.

"It's on the house."

"I can't do that," Palmer said. "I want to pay my way."

The bartender frowned.

"Whataya— Oh, I get it. You think I'm givin' it to you because you're the law? Naw. Strangers always get the first one on the house."

"Oh, well, in that case, thanks."

"Sure thing," the bartender said. "Welcome to Integrity, Marshal."

Palmer turned his back to the bar with beer in hand and took a long look at the interior of the saloon. Everybody seemed to be having a good time, either gambling, drinking, or flirting with the working girls. Unlike many saloons Palmer had been in over the years, there were no arguments or fights going on at the moment.

He turned back to the bar and waved the bartender over.

"Yeah, Marshal?"

"What's your name?"

"My name's Wade."

"Is this a typical night in here, Wade?" Palmer asked. "Quiet, with everybody having a good time?"

"You ain't gonna find no trouble in here durin' the week, Marshal," Wade said, "but weekends are different. Friday and Saturday nights the cowhands come to town, and the usual stuff happens."

"Arguments and fights?"

"That's right."

"Gunplay?"

"Not usually," Wade said. "Might be some if there's a disagreement about a woman or a poker hand, but it don't happen much. Not here, anyway."

"Is it different at other saloons?"

"I don't wanna talk bad about the competition," Wade said, "but there's one or two that have—whatchacallit—nondesirable customers?"

Palmer knew he meant "undesirable," but didn't bother to correct him. Being educated was never something he flaunted, especially considering the types of outlaws he had worked with over the years. . . .

CHAPTER SIX

SIXTEEN-YEAR-OLD TOM PALMER held the reins of the four horses while mounted on his own. He looked around nervously, feeling like everyone on the street who walked by was staring at him.

The other four members of the gang were in the bank, and there hadn't been any shots yet. That was good. Carson had told him to hold on to his nerve and to act like nothing was wrong.

"If anybody asks you what yer doin', just say yer waitin'. Got it?"

"I got it."

"You can do this, kid," Carson said. "I know ya can."

"Right," Palmer had said, "I can do it."

Jeff Carson was a forty-year-old man who had been an outlaw for more than half his life. He said he could always spot talent, and he spotted it in Tom Palmer, who at that time was an orphan.

"Your parents are dead, you had plenny of schoolin', and you're a smart kid," Carson told Palmer. "And now it's time for you to go on your first job."

It was a small bank in a small town—easy pickings, according to Carson.

"All you gotta do is hold the horses," Carson told him. "Easy. Nothin's gonna go wrong."

But it did. . . .

PALMER WOKE WITH a start. He hadn't dreamed about his first job in years, but lately it had been recurring. He figured that was because things had gone very wrong his first time out, and now things had gone wrong his last time. He had come full circle in twenty years, and now he was hoping to put that life behind him and start over as Marshal Cassidy.

He sat up in bed, swung his feet to the floor, and rubbed his face with his hands. Again, he thought he should get rid of the mustache. After washing up, he got dressed, pinned on the badge, and looked at himself in the mirror. This was his second day on the job. It was only because he knew his own past that it looked odd. Nobody else would give it a second thought.

He went downstairs to have breakfast, but as he reached the lobby, the clerk waved at him.

"Got somethin' for you, Marshal," the man said, holding an envelope.

"When did this come in?" Palmer asked, accepting it.

"Earlier this morning," the clerk said. "One of the mayor's lackeys— I mean, one of his men brought it in, told me not to wake you, just to give it to you when you came down."

"All right, thanks," Palmer said.

He took the envelope with him into the dining room, ordered his breakfast before opening the envelope. It was a note telling him about the meeting that was to take place later that evening to introduce him to the townspeople who attended. He refolded the note, put it back in the envelope, and tucked it into his shirt pocket.

After breakfast he went across the street to the barbershop.

"You're the new marshal," the barber said as he entered.

"That's right."

"What kin I do for ya?"

"I need a shave."

"They got a barber at the hotel—"

"I know," Palmer said. "He cut my hair yesterday, but I decided to give you a try with the shave. That all right?"

"It's fine with me, Marshal," the man said.

"Don't worry," Palmer said. "I'll pay for it."

"Have a seat, then," the man said. "How close you want it?"

"Pretty close," Palmer said, "and let's get rid of the mustache, too."

"You're the boss."

The barber had a lighter touch than the one at the hotel and worked very quickly.

"How's that?"

Palmer leaned forward for a look in the mirror and was quite shocked. Even he wouldn't have been able to identify himself. That was what happened when you wore a mustache and beard for so many years. He put his hand to his face and rubbed it, just to make sure it was him.

"That looks fine," he said. Palmer had noticed a sign outside that said **BATHS**. "What kind of bathtubs do you have?"

"Porcelain."

The tub Palmer had used at the hotel had been wood.

"I'll remember that for next time," he said.

"Oh, no charge, Marshal," the barber said as Palmer tried to hand him money.

"What's your name?"

"Barney."

"I'll be paying for what I get as long as I'm marshal here, Barney, so take it," Palmer said.

"Yessir."

Palmer left the barbershop, feeling not so much like a new man but certainly a different one.

P ALMER SPENT MUCH of the rest of the morning and afternoon in his office, getting it cleaned out from all the dust and grime that had built up since the last occupant left. He had cleaned the day before, but it was a two-day job. The cellblock behind the office had three cells, all of which he swept out. It felt odd for him to be inside a cell with the door wide open. That was just one of the perks of wearing a badge.

Around suppertime he went back to his hotel to eat

there, but intended to find some other restaurants or cafés in town for more variety in future meals.

As the clock approached seven p.m., he made his way to city hall for the meeting where he would be presented to some of the townspeople as their new marshal. He didn't feel comfortable that he would probably be put on display in front of them. He hoped that any nervousness on his part would be seen as normal.

As he entered, the mayor's assistant, Mrs. McQueen, was there, obviously waiting for him.

"Ah, Marshal," she said, smiling, "the mayor asked me to take you into the meeting hall."

"Lead the way, Mrs. McQueen."

As he followed her, he noticed a table in the front of the room with several chairs around it. The rest of the room was arranged with chairs for attendees. There were about twenty of them, but at the moment only three or four were being used.

When she got to the front of the room, he asked Mrs. McQueen, "What's the usual attendance for these meetings?"

"Actually, not very good," she said. "Usually the council members, but the townspeople don't normally turn out for meetings."

"Why do you think that is?" Palmer asked.

"I believe they feel they voted people in to make decisions for them, and they want to leave them to it. I expect more today, though. They'll want to have a look at you."

"That's what I'm afraid of."

She touched his arm.

"Don't be nervous. You'll do fine."

"Thank you, ma'am."

She nodded and said, "Why don't you take a seat right in front, and the mayor will ask you to stand at some point."

"I'll do that."

As it got closer to seven p.m., men and women began to file in, and Palmer realized that there would probably soon be only standing room. When Mayor O'Connor finally entered, there were three other men trailing behind him.

O'Connor approached Palmer, who stood to greet him. The mayor shook hands and introduced him to the others.

"These gentlemen are our town council," he said. "Bob Forest, Harvey Beckett, and Sam Galway."

The three men shook hands with Palmer, who found their grips distinct from one another. One was as limp as a noodle; another was moist and clammy while the third—Beckett's—was firm and strong. Beckett was a large, powerfully built man, and Palmer suspected that he was the blacksmith in town.

Forest and Galway didn't speak, just ducked their heads and sat at the table. Beckett said, "Pleasure to know you, Marshal," and then sat.

"We'll be starting in a minute," O'Connor told Palmer. "When I introduce you, I'll call you up to sit with us."

"There're only four chairs," Palmer pointed out.

"Don't worry," O'Connor said, "one of these gents will give you theirs."

"Or I could stand."

"Your choice," O'Connor said, and joined his council at the table. Palmer sat back down in the front row, where he now had a man on his left and a woman on his right. They each gave him a nod, which he returned.

"Ladies and gentlemen," O'Connor called out, "I see we have a good turnout tonight. I'm sorry there aren't enough seats, but this won't be a long town meeting." A few more people entered the room and O'Connor said, "Find a place, please. Thank you."

Palmer turned in his seat to have a look at the crowd. There were men and women of all ages, most of whom had dressed for the event. He saw only one or two men who were sporting pistols. Townspeople, all.

"All right," O'Connor shouted, and Palmer turned back to the front. "Thank you all for coming and let's get right to it. We're here to introduce and welcome our new marshal." He pointed at Palmer. "Meet Marshal Abraham Cassidy."

Palmer stood up and the crowded room treated him to a smattering of applause.

"The marshal started his new job yesterday and has taken up this position in the old sheriff's office."

"I thought we were going to build him a new office," someone called out.

"Yes," O'Connor said, "that suggestion is still under review. Marshal Cassidy is available for any questions."

"Marshal," a woman's voice called out, "we understood you were bringin' your wife and children here with you."

"I was," Palmer said, "but our wagons were attacked

soon after we crossed into South Dakota. My family was killed."

"How did you manage to survive that attack?" a man's voice asked.

Palmer hesitated, then said, "I've been wondering that myself."

CHAPTER SEVEN

I THINK THAT'S ENOUGH questions about the marshal's family," Mayor O'Connor said. "I think the man's dedication is unquestionable, considering he continued on after burying his family out on the prairie and arrived in town yesterday to take up his new job. So let's have some questions that don't have to do with that tragedy."

Palmer spent the next fifteen minutes fielding questions about what he planned to do to keep the people of the town of Integrity safe and how he hoped to help the town grow.

"All right," Mayor O'Connor said, as more hands went up, "that'll be all for now. I'm sure you'll all have time to meet the marshal around town as he's doing his job. Some of you might even want to buy him a drink or a meal—"

"Do you mind if I say something?" Palmer asked, cutting him off.

"No, of course," O'Connor said. "Go ahead."

"I won't be expecting anything free in this job," he told the assembled people. "Those of you who have businesses, I'll be paying for anything I need, whether it's a drink, a meal, or . . . a shirt. Whatever I buy, I'll be paying for."

"Well," the mayor said, "the town *will* be supplying you with a place to live."

"That's fine," Palmer said, "and I appreciate that. I just want it known that I won't be the kind of lawman who has his hand out. I've known those kinds of men . . . even back East . . . and I'm here to tell you: That's not me. Thank you for coming to welcome me tonight."

Again he was treated to a smattering of applause.

"And with that," O'Connor said, "this town meeting is adjourned."

Some people began to file out, while others came up to Palmer to shake his hand or ask one last question. When the room was finally empty, the town council members also moved past him, all giving him a nod, except for Beckett, who shook his hand.

"That was well done, Marshal."

"Thank you, Mr. Beckett."

"Especially the part about not havin' your hand out," Beckett said. "And please, in the future, just call me Harve."

"All right, Harve," Palmer said, "and you can call me—"

"I'll be callin' you 'Marshal,'" Beckett said, "because that's the respect you deserve."

Beckett left, leaving Palmer with the mayor and Mrs. McQueen.

"Well," O'Connor said, "that went well. I think you're ready to carry on."

"I had a visit from a fella named Atlee?" Palmer said. "Told me he was my deputy."

"Steve Atlee is no deputy," the mayor said. "Oh, he's volunteered for the job often enough, but believe me, he's not qualified. As for deputies, that's going to be up to you, Marshal. I assume after a few days or weeks, you'll know if you need any. When the time comes, just check in with me and we'll see what we can do."

"I'll do that," Palmer said. "Thanks, Mayor." He touched the brim of his hat and, after nodding to Mrs. McQueen, turned and left.

A man approached him as he stepped outside city hall.

"Marshal," he said, "my name's Winston, Harry Winston."

"Mr. Winston," Palmer said, "I saw you inside."

"I'm the editor of the local newspaper, the *Integrity Times*. I wonder if we might talk awhile."

"Talk, yes," Palmer said. "An interview, no."

"That's fine," Winston said. "We won't call it an interview. But I think the people who didn't attend the town meeting have a right to know what they missed."

"Just between you and me, Mr. Winston," Palmer said, "I don't think they missed a whole helluva lot."

"I think we should leave that to them, don't you?"

Palmer studied the man. He appeared to be in his forties. He was wearing a three-piece suit and a bowler hat, and he had a pencil in his hand, ready to take notes.

"Come with me to my office," Palmer said, "and we'll talk."

T HEY SPOKE FOR an hour, and each time the danger arose that it might become an interview, Palmer steered it away.

"I think people will want to know about . . . the tragedy," Winston said. "Where it happened and how."

"How does an Indian attack happen?" Palmer said. "They came rushing down on us before we even knew it. I killed two, perhaps three, and then I blacked out. When I woke, my family was all dead, the wagons burned."

"You blacked out?"

"Something must've hit me," Palmer said. "I had a bump on my head."

"They probably thought you were dead, too," the newspaperman said.

"That's what I thought," Palmer said, and then added—as he thought an Easterner might—"but I've read the stories about Indians scalping their enemies. They didn't scalp me or the others. They just left us for dead."

"Where did this happen?" Winston asked.

"I'm not gonna say," Palmer replied. "I don't want people trying to dig them up."

"But wouldn't you rather have them buried here in our cemetery?"

"They're buried where they died," Palmer said. "That's good enough."

"If you say so," Winston said.

He stood up, preparing to leave.

"If I think of any other questions, may I come and see you?"

"Why not?"

"I might be interested in . . . your level of education."

"Check with the mayor, then," Palmer suggested. "It's all in the letters we exchanged, I'm sure."

"Quite right," Winston said. "I'll do that. Thank you for your time, Marshal."

"You're welcome."

At the door the newspaper editor turned and gave the place a good long look.

"They really should get you a new office," he said.

"This'll do for now," Palmer assured him.

The newspaperman nodded and left.

With the town meeting finished and Winston satisfied, Palmer went to the stove and made a pot of coffee. He was officially on the job. . . .

P ALMER TOOK A walk around town later, looking for someplace other than his hotel to eat. He passed several people on the street who greeted him, and he touched the brim of his hat in return.

"Takin' a look at our town, Marshal?" a woman asked as she walked past him with her husband.

"My town, too, now, ma'am," he said.

"We were at the meeting, my husband and me," she said. "We were sorry to hear about your family."

"Thank you."

The handsome couple looked to be in their late thirties, but while the woman smiled and seemed friendly, the man exhibited no emotion and just stared.

They had dressed well for the meeting, seemed to still be wearing the same Sunday-go-to-meeting clothes.

"Are you lookin' for somethin' in particular?" the woman asked.

"Supper," Palmer said, "but someplace other than in my hotel."

"Oh, that's easy." She kept her right arm linked with her husband's, but pointed with her left in the direction they had just come. "The Sweetwater Steak House, two blocks that way. We just came from there ourselves. Best steaks in town."

"Thank you, Mrs. . . ."

"We're the Hendersons," the woman said. "I'm Belle. This is my husband, Ken."

"Nice to meet you both," Palmer said, "and thanks for the tip."

"Always happy to help, Marshal," Belle said.

She turned, her husband turning with her, and they continued walking.

Palmer continued on and came to the Sweetwater Steak House. There were two large picture windows in front, both with the name of the place stenciled on them.

He went inside.

BELLE HENDERSON'S RECOMMENDATION turned out to be excellent. He couldn't judge if it was the best steak in town, but it was a good one.

"No charge, Marshal," the waiter told him when he stood to leave.

"I'll pay for my meal. Thanks," Palmer said.

"Suit yerself." The waiter gave him a check and

Palmer left the money on the table. It reminded him that he didn't have much left in his poke. He was going to have to ask the mayor when he got paid. And how much. It had probably been discussed in the letters, which were in his saddlebag.

He headed back to his hotel.

I N HIS ROOM he tossed the saddlebags on the bed and took the letters out. As he studied them, he found the answers to his questions. He was to get forty a month, plus room and board. The money would be paid the first of every month, which meant he either had to ask for an advance or make the money he had last the next two weeks. He could make it by eating most of his meals in the hotel, or accepting free meals in places like the Sweetwater, which he didn't want to do. He didn't want anybody thinking they had managed to buy him. He had already told everyone at the town meeting that his hand would not be out, and he intended to stick to that.

So meals and drinks in the Utopia Hotel until he started collecting his pay.

CHAPTER EIGHT

PALMER HAD ALREADY resigned himself to the fact that he would be spending much time in his hotel dining room and saloon, when the mayor visited his office the next morning and dropped an envelope on his desk.

"This month's pay," O'Connor said. "I hope you agree you're entitled to half a month's worth."

"That's fine," Palmer said. "I was getting down to my last nickel."

"I thought that might be the case," O'Connor said, "and since you're determined to pay your way, I wanted to make sure you'd be able to."

Palmer picked the envelope up and said, "Much obliged to you, Mr. Mayor."

"Looks like you cleaned this place up," the mayor said.

"I'm a pretty good hand with a broom," Palmer told him.

O'Connor smiled. "We didn't discuss that talent in our letters, did we?"

"No, we didn't."

"Just your proficiency with a handgun."

"That seemed to be of more importance for the job," Palmer observed.

"I don't want to ask for a demonstration—"

"I don't do trick shooting, Mr. Mayor," Palmer said. "I thought our letters satisfied all your questions."

"Of course," O'Connor said. "After all, you have the job."

"Yes."

"If it turns out you can't shoot as well as you indicated—"

"That'll be my problem, won't it?" Palmer asked.

"Indeed," the mayor said. "I understand you met the Hendersons yesterday."

"That I did," Palmer said. "How did that fact get around?"

"Oh, somebody saw you talking to them on the street."

"He didn't talk much, but she steered me to the Sweetwater for supper."

"That's a good place."

"Why would you be concerned that I talked with them—that is, her?"

"I'm not, really. It's just that— Well, they own the mercantile, probably the biggest store in town. . . ."

"Ah."

"And she happens to be the one I beat for my job."

"She ran for mayor?" Palmer asked. "That's interesting. How close was the election?"

"Not close at all," O'Connor said.

"Tell me," Palmer said, "does the husband talk?"

"Quite a bit, when he has a mind to," O'Connor said.

"She's a good-looking woman," Palmer observed.

"You should also know," O'Connor said, "that Ken Henderson is a jealous man."

"I'll keep that in mind, Mr. Mayor."

"You have a good day, Marshal."

"One more thing," Palmer said. "I've been in the mercantile and I didn't see them."

"They have employees," O'Connor said, "but they're in there every so often."

"I see." Palmer held the envelope up. "Thanks again, Mr. Mayor."

After the mayor had gone, Palmer opened the envelope and counted out twenty dollars. He wasn't rich, but at least he was solvent.

He had just tucked the money into his shirt pocket when the door opened again and Steve Atlee came in.

"Mr. Atlee," Palmer said.

"Deputy Atlee, right?" the man said. "Did you make up your mind?"

"Not at all," Palmer said. "It's going to take me a few days, maybe longer."

"But you're the marshal," Atlee said. "You can hire anybody you want."

"Can I?" Palmer asked. "How come I didn't see you at the meeting last night?"

Atlee made a face.

"They wouldn't want me there."

"They? Who?"

"The town council," Atlee said. "And the mayor." He made a face. "Especially the mayor."

"Yes," Palmer said, "I have to admit he didn't have anything nice to say about you."

"He wouldn't."

"Why not?"

"He hates me."

"Why?"

"Ask 'im," Atlee said, then turned and left.

Aside from the young man being a little too anxious to be a deputy, Palmer couldn't see anything objectionable about Steve Atlee. When it came time for him to hire deputies—if that time came—he'd have to ask the mayor for specific reasons why he didn't want Steve Atlee wearing a badge.

The office filled with the smell of coffee and Palmer rose and poured himself a cup, carried it back to his desk, and took his time drinking it.

M AYOR O'CONNOR LOOKED up when the door to his office opened.

"How did you get past Mrs. McQueen, Rogan?" he asked.

Ben Rogan walked to the chair in front of the mayor's desk and sat. He stretched his long legs out in front of him, pushed his hat back on his head with his forefinger.

"Mr. Waverly sent me."

"Why wasn't the owner of the biggest ranch in the territory at the town meeting to meet the new marshal?" O'Connor asked.

"He was busy."

"He could've sent you."

"I was busy, too," Rogan said. "What's he like?"

O'Connor scowled.

"He's not like what I thought he'd be from his letters," he admitted. "He's too . . . calm, too assured. Especially for a man who's just lost his family."

"Lost?"

O'Connor explained to Rogan that the marshal's family had been killed by Indians.

"And they left him alive?"

"That's another thing that doesn't make sense," O'Connor said. "An Easterner should be dead, because he killed himself after his family was murdered. Instead, he walked into town calm as you please to take up his job."

"He may just be that kind of man," Rogan said. "Mr. Waverly wants to know if he's gonna be hard to handle?"

"So far he says he wants no handouts," O'Connor said, "but he's taking the room and board, so I think he'll come around."

"Deputies?"

"None yet," O'Connor said.

"Is he gonna have any volunteers?"

"He's had one," the mayor said. "Steve Atlee."

"Atlee," Rogan said derisively. "He ain't no deputy."

"That's what I told our new marshal."

Rogan stood up. He had been the Bar W foreman for five years, since Franklin Waverly bought his spread. Approaching forty, Rogan was Waverly's right hand, and he had all of the Bar W ranch hands under his thumb.

"I'll tell Mr. Waverly what you had to say," Rogan said. "He'll probably wanna see you at some point."

"He can come to town, or I'll go and see him," O'Connor said. "Whatever he chooses."

"Oh, he's gonna want you to come out there as soon as ya can."

"All right," O'Connor said, "tell him I'll be out later today."

Rogan nodded and left.

O'Connor sat back in his chair as Ben Rogan left his office. He had known Waverly was going to want to see him after the new marshal arrived. He opened his top drawer and took out all the letters Abraham Cassidy had written him and started reading them again. . . .

P ALMER DECIDED HE'D make rounds in the afternoon and in the evening: in the afternoon to let Integrity's citizens know he was on the job, and in the evening to make sure all the businesses and homes were safe and secure. And in the evenings, he could also check in with all the saloons and be sure things were going smoothly. He figured he'd run into some troublesome drunks, but that was to be expected. And he had seen enough of those encounters in countless saloons to know how to handle them.

During his afternoon rounds, he didn't run into another friendly face like that of Belle Henderson. Most of the people either ignored him or gave him a nod, and both suited him just fine.

Thinking of the Hendersons, he decided to make their mercantile store one of the businesses he would pop his head into just to make an appearance. As he did, he was pleased to see Belle behind the counter, and her husband nowhere to be found.

"Marshal," she said as he entered, "how nice."

He took a better look at Belle today. Not bundled up in a coat, he saw that she was much more than just a handsome woman. She was actually quite lovely and well formed. Why would her husband walk down the street with a sour look on his face when he had this woman on his arm?

"Just thought I'd stop in and make sure everything was all right, Mrs. Henderson. Or should I just call you Miz Belle?"

"I tell you what," she said, leaning on the counter in what he could describe only as a flirtatious manner, "why don't you just call me Belle?"

"As long as it's all right with your husband," he replied.

"Oh, pooh," she said, "don't you worry about Ken. You and I can become good friends without his say-so."

Yes, he thought, *very flirtatious.*

"Would you like to stay for a cup of tea?" she asked. "Or something stronger?"

"I'm afraid I'm making my rounds, Belle," he said. "I have to let the citizens know I'm on the job."

"Well, there's a chill in the air," she said, "so come back anytime for something . . . warm."

He touched the brim of his hat and left the mercantile, aware that this was the kind of brazen woman he was going to have to be careful of.

CHAPTER NINE

Mayor O'Connor drove his buggy out to the Bar W, a huge, sprawling spread with a large two-story house, a big red barn, a corral, and a bunkhouse. He stopped the buggy in front of the house and a few of the hands drifted over from the corral.

"Take a look, boys," one of them said. "The mayor's here."

There were three of them, all in their early thirties, wearing faded work clothes covered with sweat stains despite the cold.

"I'm looking for Rogan," the mayor said. "Is he around?"

"Whataya want 'im for?" one man asked.

"He came to my office and asked me to drive out here," O'Connor said. "Here I am."

"He's in the barn," the spokesman said. He looked at one of the other men. "Go get 'im."

"Right."

That man turned and trotted off to the barn.

"We got us a sick bull givin' us fits," the spokesman told the mayor.

"Sorry to hear it," O'Connor said.

"We heard the new marshal got into town."

"That's right. Started his job a few days ago."

"Good man?"

"We'll see," O'Connor said, "won't we?"

"I guess we'll meet 'im when we come to town Saturday night."

"Not to make trouble, I hope," the mayor said.

"Make trouble?" He looked at his friend, who was grinning. "Us? We're just gonna have a few drinks and blow off a little steam, Mr. Mayor."

O'Connor saw the third man come out of the barn, followed by Ben Rogan.

"You boys get back to the barn, keep an eye on that bull," Rogan snapped.

"Sure, boss."

The three men walked back toward the barn.

"You can leave your buggy right there," Rogan said. "The boss said he wanted to see you as soon as you got here."

"Fine."

O'Connor stepped down, tied the horses off, then followed Rogan up the stairs to the front door. Franklin Waverly had made sure when he built the house that it was the largest one in the county.

Rogan led O'Connor into the entry hall and said, "Wait here."

"I thought he was expecting me."

"Let me see where he is," Rogan said. "Just wait here."

The foreman disappeared into the house, came back about five minutes later.

"Come on, he's in the back."

Rogan led O'Connor through the house to a large room in the back. The walls were lined with books, and there was a large desk in front of a window that looked out the back. Franklin Waverly was behind the desk. He sat back in his chair as the two men entered.

"Ben, get the mayor a drink," Waverly said. "Sherry?"

"Sure," O'Connor said.

"Have a seat, Victor," Waverly invited.

O'Connor sat down.

Waverly was a well-groomed sixty, with a full head of gray hair and a beard to match. He had sharp blue eyes that were clear as a bell, and when he moved, it was with a vitality that belied his years. Some of that energy might have been generated by his wife, who was twenty years younger than he was.

Rogan handed his boss a glass of sherry, and then the mayor.

"Okay, thanks, Ben. You'd better get back to that bull."

"Yes, sir."

Rogan left the room.

"So," Waverly said, "Ben tells me the new marshal's in town."

"You know he is," O'Connor said. "I asked you to come to the town meeting to welcome him."

"I was a little busy. But you can tell me what I missed."

"A passel of nonsense questions from the town," O'Connor said.

"I heard something about him losing his family."

"He says they were attacked by Indians, and when he woke up, his family was dead."

"All of them?"

"Yes."

"Why'd they leave him alive?"

"He wonders that, too," O'Connor said.

"What do you think?"

"Something doesn't feel right," O'Connor said.

"Why?"

"He's too calm for a man who's suffered such a loss," O'Connor said.

"Where did he say it happened?" Waverly asked.

"He didn't," O'Connor said.

"Doesn't he want somebody to go back there and bring the bodies here for a decent burial?"

"He says no," O'Connor said. "He wants to leave them where they are."

Waverly tapped his forefinger against the side of the glass he was holding.

"That does sound odd."

O'Connor sipped his sherry. Waverly, a wealthy man, had the best of everything in his house. And he had chosen O'Connor as the best candidate for the job of mayor of Integrity, and gotten him elected. For that, O'Connor felt he owed the man, but Waverly felt he owned the mayor.

"We're going to have to keep an eye on him," Waverly said. "We'll have to watch how he performs and wait and see if he'll play along."

"With what?" O'Connor asked.

Waverly gave the mayor a stone-faced look and said, "Whatever."

* * *

WHEN O'CONNOR CAME out, no one was near his buggy. He looked across the way at the corral, which was empty. He assumed the men were all in the barn, tending to the sick bull, or off somewhere else doing their jobs. He untied his horse, climbed into the seat of the buggy, and headed back to town.

PALMER WAS JUST about to begin his evening rounds when he saw the mayor driving back into town in his buggy. He stopped walking, and as the man drove by, they exchanged touches to their hat brims. He wondered what business the politician had been out of town taking care of.

But that really wasn't his business, was it? He had a job to do, and he was going to start doing it and seeing how things progressed. He knew there was always the possibility that he'd have to leave town, especially if he got recognized, but at the moment, he was feeling fairly safe in his new identity.

After exchanging greetings with the mayor, he crossed the street and began walking. It was dusk and most of the shops were closed, except for a couple of cafés and the hotel and saloons.

So far the only saloons he had been in were the one connected to his hotel and the Palomino, so he decided that tonight he'd make an appearance at the others, however many there were.

The first one he came to was the Silver Spur. Just outside the batwing doors, he could hear piano music, chips striking chips, laughter from women, and shouts from men. It was obviously a busy place—one that a town marshal should pay attention to.

He went through the swinging doors and entered.

L OOKEE THERE," BRAZOS Lane said to his three friends. They were all seated at a table with beer mugs and a bottle of whiskey in front of them. They had started drinking early, before the saloon got so crowded, before the piano player and the girls had come down, and they were very drunk at the moment.

"What?" Jelly Reynolds asked, looking around.

"There, at the door," Lane said. "That look like a man wearin' a badge to you?"

Jelly blinked and squinted and said, "Well, yeah, it does. A marshal's badge, if I ain't blind."

"Wasn't there a new marshal comin' to town?" Lane asked.

"Seems I heard somethin' about that," Jelly said.

The other two men weren't listening to the conversation. They were arguing about who was going to walk to the bar for more beers.

"Hey," Lane said to them, "hey, shut the hell up!"

The two men shut their mouths and looked at Lane. They were all friends, but it was Lane who usually decided what they were going to do.

"I'll get the beers," Lane said. "You fellas just sit tight and follow my lead, ya hear?"

Jelly and the other two nodded and tried to get one last sip out of their glasses as Brazos Lane stood up and headed for the bar.

CHAPTER TEN

PALMER WAS AWARE he was drawing some looks as the new lawman in town. When he got to the crowded bar, a space opened for him and he bellied up. The bartender, a beefy man in his fifties, saw him and lumbered over.

"So you're the new law?" he asked.

"That's me," Palmer said. "Marshal Cassidy."

"Pleased to meetcha, Marshal," the man said. "Folks around here just call me Skinny."

"Really? Why's that?"

"Because up until the time I turned fifty, I *was* skinny," the man said. "That was a few years ago, and I been packin' on the pounds ever since. What can I getcha?"

"A beer, thanks."

"Comin' up."

When Skinny served him his beer, Palmer noticed

more than a few eyes on him. He assumed they were going to judge him according to the way he drank it, so he proceeded to pour half of it down his gullet and then wipe his mouth on his shirtsleeve. That seemed to satisfy most that he was going to be one of them.

"Lively place," Palmer said.

"Come back in a coupla nights," Skinny said. "Saturdays are crazy here. This is just kinda a normal weeknight."

"I'll keep that in mind. What do you have in the way of house tables?"

"Just one for faro and one for blackjack."

"No poker?"

"That's up to the customers," Skinny said. "If they wanna start up a game, they can go ahead."

"You take a cut?"

"Just from the house games."

"I see."

"You know," Skinny said, "there's gonna be them that wants to try you out."

"I figure."

"Especially when they're drunk."

"Are you trying to tell me not to be in saloons?" Palmer asked.

"No," Skinny said, "I'm just tellin' you it might be startin' right now."

Palmer looked in the mirror behind the bar and saw a man coming toward him.

"Thanks for the warning," Palmer said.

Skinny moved on down the bar and Palmer turned to face the approaching man. He was in his thirties, dressed in work clothes, with a pistol tucked into his belt worn for a left-handed draw.

"So you're the new marshal in town?" the man said.

"That's right."

"That's interestin'," he said. "My friends and me was just sayin' how interestin' that is."

"Your friends?"

The man turned and pointed to a table with three men seated at it.

"Are they as drunk as you are?" Palmer asked.

"Nearly," the man said.

"What's your name?"

"They call me Brazos Lane."

"Why Brazos?"

"Because I don't like my real first name," Lane said.

"What is it?"

Lane made a face and said, "George."

"You're right," Palmer said. "That's terrible."

"Buy you a drink, Marshal?"

"Sorry," Palmer said, holding up his half-filled mug. "One's my limit while I'm making my rounds."

"I see you wear your gun in one of them holsters," Lane said.

"I like the way it feels," Palmer said.

"Me, I prefer it right here," Lane said, patting his weapon, "so I can feel it against my belly."

"As long as you don't draw it, we'll be fine," Palmer said. "In fact, I'm thinking of starting a no-guns-within-the-city-limits law."

Lane laughed.

"You think you can do that?" he asked.

"I'm the law, remember."

"Yeah," Lane said, "you're the law as long as you do what they want you to do."

"That wasn't the deal."

"Yeah, well, you'll find out what the deal is."

"Who are you, anyway?" Palmer asked. "What do you do?"

"Me and my partners," Lane said, "we're for hire."

"Guns?"

Lane shrugged.

"Guns, trackin', buildin' a barn, deliverin' mail, whatever needs to be done. This town don't run so good without us."

"Uh-huh."

"You'll find out, Marshal," Lane said. "I just wanted to introduce myself."

"And your partners?"

"Their names don't matter," Lane said. "Anybody needs us, they deal with me. In fact, if you ever need deputies—"

"I haven't made up my mind about that yet," Palmer said.

"Ah, well," Lane said, "when ya do, just keep us in mind."

"I'll do that."

Lane studied Palmer for a few moments, then asked, "You any good with that gun?"

"I've been known to hit what I'm aiming at," Palmer said.

"Fast?"

"Not especially."

Lane laughed.

"Why do I get the feelin' you ain't tellin' the whole truth?" he asked.

"Who tells the whole truth?" Palmer asked.

"You got that right," Lane said. "I'm just gonna get some fresh beers for me and my friends."

"Go right ahead."

"Skinny!" Lane called out. "Four more."

Skinny set four full ones on the bar. Lane grabbed them and carried them to the table. Palmer watched, then turned back to the bar. But he made sure he could see the table in the mirror.

"Hired guns?" he asked Skinny.

"Sometimes," Skinny said. "Mostly they do odd jobs around town, like he said. But they think they can handle anybody and anythin'. If I was you, I'd watch 'em. Sooner or later, they're gonna wanna try you."

"They all do what George tells them to do?"

Skinny laughed at Palmer's use of Brazos Lane's real name.

"Pretty much."

"So he's the one I need to watch."

"You got it."

Palmer finished his beer, set down the empty mug, and tossed a coin on the bar.

"What about the other saloons in town?"

"Not as big as this one," Skinny said, "but we're all pretty busy. Except the one in the hotel. That's pretty much just for guests. You gonna check them all out?"

"I thought I'd at least take a look at them," Palmer said.

"Well, you got the Palomino, the Last Chance, and the Little Dakota. They're down the street. Ya can't miss 'em."

"Any smaller ones off the main street?" Palmer asked.

"Not really. But the town's growin'. There's gonna be more."

"And the restaurants in town? They all serve liquor?"

"Beer with supper," Skinny said. "No whiskey."

"Good to know," Palmer said. "Thanks, Skinny."

"Anytime, Marshal."

Palmer took one last look at the table with Lane and his partners; Lane looked over at him and nodded. Palmer nodded back and left.

One down, two to go . . .

H E HIT THE Last Chance next.
It was smaller than the Silver Spur, but seemed to be doing as brisk a business. Once again he attracted attention as he entered and approached the bar.

"What brings you in, Marshal?" the tall, skinny bartender asked.

"Just making my rounds," Palmer said.

"You gonna be doin' that every night?"

"Pretty much."

"Lookin' for trouble?"

"I hope not."

"Well, there ain't any in here," the man said. "Most of these are repeat customers, and they know I don't stand for no trouble."

"That's good to know," Palmer said.

"You want a drink?"

"No, thanks," Palmer said. "Like I said, just came in for a look-see."

He turned his back to the bar, saw that most of the tables were taken. There were a couple of girls in brightly colored gowns working the floor, but unlike the Spur, no piano, no music.

Palmer turned back to the bartender.

"You run any house games?"

"No, sir," the bartender said. "I leave the gamblin' up to the customers."

"Understood," Palmer said.

"You been to the other saloons?"

"The Palomino and the Spur," Palmer said. "I'm going to the Little Dakota after this."

"Well, watch out for that one."

"Why's that?"

"Let's just say they cater to more of the undesirables in town."

"Undesirables?" Palmer repeated. "That's a pretty big word for a bartender."

"When I first came here," the man said, "I was a schoolteacher."

"What happened?"

"No more school."

"This town," Palmer said, "that's supposed to be growing, has no school?"

"It does now, but by the time they opened it, I was working here."

"So?"

The man shrugged.

"I like it. And they hired themselves a schoolmarm."

"What's your name?"

The man grinned.

"What's that matter?" he asked. "Folks in here just call me Bartender."

"Well, Bartender," Palmer said, "I'm Marshal Cassidy."

"Pleased to know you, Marshal."

"How do things usually go in here?"

"Peaceful. Like I said, the place you've got to look out for is the Dakota."

"I'll have to go over there and find out for myself," Palmer said.

"You do that," the bartender said. "Just be careful. If you can handle yourself, you should be all right."

"I've lived this long," Palmer said.

"Well, let's hope being the lawman here, you live a lot longer."

"I'm going to do my best," Palmer said. "Thanks, Bartender."

CHAPTER ELEVEN

H E WALKED TO the Little Dakota.

As he entered he noticed several things. First, it wasn't as clean as the other two places. Second, it wasn't as busy. Third, there were no girls working the floor. Maybe that was part of the reason why it wasn't as busy.

As he walked in, the energy level noticeably lowered. There were men sitting at tables with their heads bowed, almost resting on their drinks. For that reason he didn't have as many eyes on him when he approached the bar, except for the tired-looking bartender, who seemed as if he had been behind the bar for forty years.

"Evenin'," Palmer greeted the old barman.

Rheumy, faded eyes squinted at the badge on his chest.

"Is that for real?" he asked in a scratchy voice.

"It is," Palmer said. "I'm Marshal Cassidy."

"Since when?" the bartender asked.

"Well," Palmer answered, "let's say starting now."

"So you want a beer?"

"No, thanks," Palmer said. "I'm making my rounds, is all."

"So you'll be in here every night at this time?" the bartender asked.

"Let's say every night," Palmer said, "but not necessarily at the same time. I wouldn't want to become predictable."

The bartender snickered.

"Stay alive longer if ya don't," he agreed.

"Is this how business usually is here?" Palmer asked.

"Pretty much, 'cept maybe Saturday night."

"Yeah, that's what I've been hearing," Palmer said. "Well, I'll be through here on Saturday night, just to have a look-see."

"And you'll be welcome," the bartender said. "I got nothin' a-gin the law."

"That's good to hear."

"'Course, I can't say the same for them's that drink in here."

"That's what I figured," Palmer said. "You have a good night."

"Thanks, Marshal."

Palmer left the Little Dakota and continued his rounds.

H E FINISHED CHECKING the doors of all the closed businesses to make sure they were firmly locked, then went back down the main street one more time.

As he approached the mercantile, he decided to try the door again. When he did, he became aware of somebody in the shadows sitting in a chair.

"Evenin', Sheriff," Ken Henderson greeted him.

"Mr. Henderson," Palmer said. "Didn't notice you there at first. Do you usually sit out here in front of your store?"

"Only when I think somebody might be interested in my wife," Henderson said.

"And who might that be?" Palmer asked.

Henderson stood up. He was a tall man, but Palmer wasn't too concerned since he wasn't armed.

"You usually check the same place more than once when you're makin' your rounds, Marshal?" the man asked. "Maybe you thought the door would be . . . unlocked for you?"

"Let me get this straight," Palmer said. "You think I'm interested in your wife?"

"Why wouldn't you be?" Henderson asked. "She's a good-lookin' woman."

"Mr. Henderson," Palmer said, "there might be some men in this town who are interested in her, but I'm not one of them. I just came here to start my new job, and in case you haven't heard, I lost my wife and family to Indians on the way here. So I'm not looking for a new woman right now."

Henderson blinked and took a step back.

"Lost your wife?"

"They killed her and my children."

"Jesus—"

"So I'm just here making sure your door is locked and your store is safe." Palmer reached for the doorknob, hoping it wouldn't turn. He doubted Belle Henderson would leave it unlocked for him, even though she had been flirting with him. But if she flirted with him, she must have done the same with other men, and maybe she'd left the door unlocked for one of them.

He tried the knob and found it locked.

"There you go," he said, removing his hand from it. "You have a nice evening."

He left the other man there with his mouth open, hopefully feeling like a fool.

B ACK IN HIS office, Palmer sat at his desk with a cup of coffee. He wasn't sure what to do next. Supper seemed to be the thing to do, but since he didn't have a deputy, did that mean he'd have to lock the office?

He'd had plenty of experiences with lawmen in his life, but usually it was because they were chasing him. He didn't know if sheriffs and marshals locked their doors or what they did after they finished their day. He assumed, like any other business, that when he was done and went to his hotel room, he should lock the office. But when was a lawman done for the day? Was he on call all the time, much like a doctor would be?

Since he couldn't ask anybody these questions without raising suspicions that he had never been a lawman before, he was just going to have to make up his own mind and stick to his decision no matter what anybody said. He was going to be Marshal Abe Cassidy, a man who had his own way of doing things.

He left the office to go have supper, and locked the door behind him.

* * *

H E DINED AT the Sweetwater Steak House because
Belle Henderson had been right about it. While
he ate his steak, he thought about her. Ken was right:
She was a very good-looking woman, and under other
circumstances, Palmer might have been interested in
her, especially since she was a flirt. But he was supposed to be a man who had just suffered the death of
his wife at the hands of the Indians. How would it look
for him to pursue another woman so soon after, and a
married one at that?

He knew he had to try not to do the things Tom
Palmer would normally have done, and figure out what
was normal for Abe Cassidy.

The waitress put his plate down in front of him, set
down the mug of beer, and then stepped back.

"Anything else I can get ya, Marshal?" the woman
asked. She was thick waisted and in her fifties; she had
probably been in Integrity all her life.

"Has this town always been called Integrity?"

"Oh, no," she said.

"Can you sit a minute?"

She looked around at the other tables. For the moment, all the diners seemed satisfied, so she pulled out
the chair across from him and sat.

"What can I do for you, Marshal?"

"What's your name?"

"Alice."

"Tell me about the town, Alice," he said, cutting
into the venison steak. "Give me some history about
the place and the people."

"The town used to be called Oakwood," she said.

"There are only a few of us left who were born here. Everybody else moved here in the last twenty years."

"What about Mayor O'Connor?"

"He's new," Alice said. "He came here five years ago."

"And he's mayor already?"

"And he's the one who changed the town's name," she said. "We became Integrity when he became mayor."

"The town went along with that?"

Alice shrugged.

"They voted him in," she said. "He promised the town would grow. So far, it has. Bringing you in was supposed to be part of that."

"Me?"

"Well, a lawman," she said. "It just happens to be you."

"O'Connor's a politician," Palmer said. "They usually have somebody behind them supporting them, financing them."

"That's right," she said. "It's most likely Mr. Waverly."

"Waverly?"

"He's the biggest rancher in the territory," Alice said. "The richest."

"And when did he come here?"

"Just after O'Connor," she said. "I think that's why he backed his campaign, because they were both newcomers."

"Did you have a lawman before me?"

"Oh, yeah," she said, "an old-timer named Kendrick. But O'Connor wanted a new man, somebody who wouldn't do things the Old West way."

"And he chose me," Palmer said.

"There was somethin' in your letters," she said.

"How do you know that?"

"I went to the town meetings where he talked about candidates. He said you were the most qualified."

"In what way?"

"You don't know?" she asked.

"I'd like to know what it was in my letters that appealed to him."

"Waitress," somebody called.

She turned and looked.

"I gotta go back to work."

As she stood up, he said, "Just tell me one thing that stood out to him."

"He said you had knowledge of the law. He said your justice wouldn't be the old-time justice of the gun."

"Okay," he said, "thanks."

"Lemme know if I can get you anything else, Marshal," she said. "Enjoy your meal."

Thanks to Alice he now knew some things he hadn't known before. Most important, he—as Cassidy—was supposed to have some knowledge of the law. Did that mean Cassidy had been a lawman back East? Or that he had studied the law? Could the real Cassidy have been a lawyer?

Palmer realized he was going to have to go through the letters he had again and read every word. He couldn't afford to have Mayor O'Connor doubting him. He was just going to have to put his best Abe Cassidy foot forward.

CHAPTER TWELVE

THE NEXT MORNING Palmer was sitting in his office, thinking about the letters he had read the night before. He had to leave them in his room. He couldn't bring them to the office and get caught reading them there. And he had to remember that he had only the letters that had gone one way, from the mayor to Abe Cassidy. He had no idea what Cassidy had written to the mayor. He could only guess. . . .

When the door opened, he almost expected to see Steve Atlee again volunteering for deputy duty. But it wasn't Atlee or anyone else Palmer knew. It was a tall, rangy man wearing work clothes, worn boots, a black hat, and no gun. Obviously a cowhand.

"Are you Marshal Cassidy, the new lawman here?" the man asked.

"That's right. I am," Palmer replied. "What can I do for you?"

"My name's Rogan, Marshal," the man said. "I'm the foreman out at the Bar W ranch."

"Okay."

Rogan smiled.

"Since you're new around here you probably don't know about—"

"Mr. Waverly?"

"Then you *have* heard of him."

"The richest man in the county?" Palmer asked. "Yeah, I have."

"Well, the boss sent me into town to invite you to have lunch with him at his house."

"Why?" Palmer asked.

"I reckon he just wantsta get to know the new lawman in town," Rogan said.

"You sure he doesn't want to see if he can buy me?" Palmer asked.

Rogan frowned.

"That's a little out of line, ain't it, Marshal?" the foreman asked.

"Maybe it is," Palmer admitted. "Tell Mr. Waverly I accept. When would he like me out there?"

"How does noon suit ya?"

"Just fine," Palmer said. "Tell Mr. Waverly I'll see him at noon."

"I'll do that, Marshal. Do you know how to get to the ranch?"

"No, I don't."

Rogan gave Palmer directions on how to get to the Bar W, then touched the brim of his hat and left the office.

Palmer wondered if he should stop in and see the mayor first, get some idea of how to handle Waverly. But on the other hand, the rancher had backed O'Connor's campaign, so the two were obviously in bed together. Palmer decided to go in cold and get his own reading on the man. It would probably be very interesting.

B EN ROGAN RODE directly back to the ranch to relay the marshal's acceptance to his boss.

"How did he take it?" Waverly asked.

"He wondered if you were gonna try to buy him."

Waverly grinned wolfishly.

"Smart man," the rancher said. "I'm sure as hell going to feel him out and see if he's for sale. What do you think of him, Ben?"

"He doesn't seem like an out-of-place dude from the East to me," Rogan said. "He's too . . . comfortable."

"That's something the mayor mentioned, too," Waverly said. "I'm going to have to get my own reading on our new lawman. Rogan, do me a favor and tell the cook I want her to go all out for the marshal."

"Yessir."

"Oh, and, Rogan?"

"Yessir?"

"You won't be joining us for lunch."

"I didn't think I would, sir."

"Like I said," Waverly went on, "I'll need to get my own reading on the man. For that, I'll need it to be just him and me."

"I get it, boss," Rogan said.

"Good man."

Rogan left to give the cook the message. Waverly sat back in his chair, then swiveled it around so he could look out the window at his holdings.

PALMER WENT TO the livery stable to see what kind of shape his horse was in. The hostler there was an old geezer named Lionel. Palmer was willing to bet that, as Alice had told him, he was one of those few people who had lived there all their lives.

"The mayor tol' me ta give you any horse you want," Lionel said. "The one you rode in on is still kinda wore out."

"What have you got, Lionel?"

"I got a good solid six-year-old mare, a five-year-old gelding, and an eight-year-old dun."

"I'll take the gelding," Palmer said. "Can you saddle him up for me?"

"'Course I can," Lionel snapped. "I'm old. I ain't crippled."

Palmer waited outside as the old man saddled his new mount. He didn't watch, for fear the hostler would think he was waiting for him to stumble. Eventually, Lionel walked the gelding out; it wore Palmer's saddle.

"Much obliged, Lionel," Palmer said.

"Where ya headed?"

"The Bar W," Palmer said. "How long a ride is that?"

"'Bout a half hour."

"Well," Palmer said, "I've got an hour to kill, so I guess I'll just get acquainted with my new buddy here. Has he got a name?"

"Nope," Lionel said. "Don't hold with namin' horses."

"Why's that?"

"In the old days," Lionel said, "ya never knew when you was gonna hafta eat one."

"Well, then," Palmer said, "I'm just going to go ahead and call him Buddy."

"Suit yerself, Marshal," Lionel said. "He's yore horse now."

"Let's go, Buddy!" Palmer said, and gave the gelding his heels.

H E TOOK A good half hour just to ride the gelding so they could get used to each other, and then he headed for the Bar W ranch. When he came within sight of it, he reined in to have a look. It was an impressive layout, with a large, imposing two-story house in the center. On one side were a barn and corral, and on the other a bunkhouse. There was a third building, which Palmer assumed was a mess hall for the hands.

"Let's go, Buddy," he said, urging the gelding into a walk. "We've got lunch waiting for us."

As he rode up to the house, he was met by three cowhands.

"Take your horse, Marshal?" one asked.

"Sure, thanks."

Another one said, "The boss is waitin' on ya. He said to go on in."

"Obliged to you," Palmer said.

The third man didn't say a word, just walked away with the one leading Palmer's horse to the barn.

"Where's Rogan?" Palmer asked the remaining hand.

"I think he might be checking out the fence line in the north pasture," the man said.

"Oh," Palmer said. "Well, thanks."

"Sure thing. We'll have your horse ready for ya when you come out."

Palmer went up the steps to the front door, wondered if he should knock first, even if he was expected. He decided he was getting the royal treatment, so he simply opened the door and entered.

"There you are," Rogan said, standing just inside. "It's almost noon."

"I know," Palmer said, surprised to see the foreman. "I'm on time."

"This way," Rogan said. "Mr. Waverly's waiting in the dining room."

Palmer followed Rogan across the large expanse of tiled entry hall, through a double doorway into a room dominated by a long wooden table. At the far end of it, a man sat.

"Boss, this is Marshal Cassidy," Rogan said. "Marshal, this is Franklin Waverly."

"You're prompt," Waverly said. "I like that."

As the man stood to shake hands, Palmer figured him for sixty or so, but his blue eyes were the clearest and sharpest he had ever seen. This man saw everything and processed it quickly. That was probably why he was rich.

As they shook hands, Waverly said, "Welcome to Integrity, Marshal, and to my home. Thank you for accepting my invitation."

"I appreciate it, Mr. Waverly," Palmer said. "I figured we'd have to meet sooner or later. Why not sooner?"

"Why not, indeed? Please, sit."

Waverly walked back to the head of the table. Palmer had his pick of many chairs, including one at the opposite end. He thought about sitting there, but decided it would have been silly. They'd have to yell at each other to be heard. In the end he went and sat in the chair to Waverly's left.

"Thank you, Ben," Waverly said. "That will be all. Let the cook know she can serve, please."

"Yessir."

Rogan went into the kitchen and didn't come back out. The next time the door opened, a stout woman wearing an apron came through, carrying steaming plates.

"This is my cook, Mrs. Butler. Best cook in the county."

She set the plates on the table wordlessly and went back to the kitchen. Palmer noticed she never looked at her boss or cracked a smile.

"Go ahead, help yourself," Waverly said.

"Thank you."

The plates held chicken and beef, and he took a bit of each, along with vegetables.

"The mayor tells me you're very qualified for this job," Waverly said.

"That's what I was hoping when I answered the ad," Palmer said.

"What's your background in the law?"

"It's all in the letters I exchanged with Mayor O'Connor," Palmer said.

"I'm sure it is," Waverly said. "I just wanted to hear it from you . . . Marshal."

Palmer looked at the untouched food on his plate. He wondered if he'd still get to eat it if he didn't answer the man's questions.

"What's your interest, Mr. Waverly?"

"Let's just say I'm nosy." The rancher smiled. "Go ahead, eat. You don't have to answer all my questions. I just wanted to get acquainted."

"I heard you're fairly new to the area," Palmer said, biting into the chicken.

"That's true," Waverly said, "but I didn't come from the East like you did. I came from California."

"Oh? What'd you do there?"

"I made money," Waverly said. "That's what I've always done. I was even in South America for a while."

"You've seen a lot of places," Palmer said. "Why this little town?"

Waverly took some beer and said, "This little town is going to grow, Marshal. Hopefully, you'll be part of that."

"I've only been here a couple of days," Palmer said. "I guess we'll have to see."

"You don't seem like an Easterner."

"Don't I?"

"They're usually all duded up," Waverly said. "You look comfortable in your clothes, and with that gun. And you don't sound like an Easterner."

"I'm trying to fit in. And they have guns in the East, Mr. Waverly," Palmer said.

"I'm sure they do," Waverly said. "Tell me, what side of the law did you get your experience from?"

"If I don't answer that," Palmer said, "can I still take another piece of chicken?"

"Sure," Waverly said, "all you want. Only why wouldn't you want to answer the question?"

"Like I said," Palmer replied, "the answers are in the letters. And I understand you and the mayor are close. I'm sure he'd show them to you."

"Could it be you just don't like to talk about yourself?" Waverly asked.

"Sure, that could be it," Palmer said. "It could also be I don't think it's any of your business."

Waverly's face became grim.

"Now there's no need to get pushy, Marshal."

"Mr. Waverly," Palmer said, "let's put our cards on the table. You invited me here to have a look at the new lawman, see if maybe I'm for sale. I accepted so I could look you over. I heard you were the richest man in the county."

"Not just the county," Waverly said.

"Well, seeing this spread, I believe it," Palmer said. "And I should tell you that I'm not for sale, not at any price."

This time Waverly smiled.

"It's my experience that when a man says 'not at any price,' he's usually just driving the price up."

Palmer hesitated a moment. There was a time in his life when he would have been trying to drive the price up. But now he was striving to be a good, decent man. But if Waverly offered him enough, would he actually be able to turn it down? Or would he revert to the man he used to be? He figured the time might come when he had to find that out. But for now . . .

"Those are probably smart businessmen that you've dealt with," Palmer said. "I'm not a smart business-man. I'm just a lawman."

Waverly studied Palmer for a few moments, then pointed and said, "Have some more of that beef. I told Mrs. Butler to go all out for you."

CHAPTER THIRTEEN

Aﬆﬄer lunch Waverly invited Palmer into his
study for a cigar. The room was lined with book-
shelves, which were filled with books. Some of their
lunch exchange had become tense, but the man still
seemed calm as he held a flame to both cigars. His
hands trembled from neither temper nor age.

"I'm thinking people don't usually talk to you the
way I did over lunch," Palmer said. "And yet here you
are, offering me a cigar."

"I respect you, Marshal," Waverly said. "If you were
easy to buy, I wouldn't."

"How about I'm impossible to buy?" Although he
still wasn't altogether sure that was true. After all,
twenty years on the outlaw trail . . .

"Let's not be hasty," the rancher and businessman
said. "There's always room for discussion."

"Discussion, yes," Palmer said. "Any sort of bribe? No."

"Now, Marshal, let's not be hasty."

"Mr. Waverly," Palmer said, "I thank you for the lunch and the cigar, but I need to get back to town. I'm on the clock, you know? Work hours?"

"All right, Marshal," Waverly said, "we'll do it your way for now. But we'll be seeing a lot of each other in the future."

"I'll always be cordial, Mr. Waverly," Palmer said. "Good afternoon."

Palmer left the study and headed for the front door. Nobody tried to stop him or show him the way.

A FTER PALMER LEFT the study, Rogan came to the door.

"Everythin' okay, boss?" he asked.

"I'm not sure," Waverly said. "I think I agree with O'Connor. This man doesn't seem like a dude from the East."

"Whataya wanna do, boss?" Rogan asked. "Get rid of 'im?"

"No, no, nothing like that," Waverly said. "I'll just have to work on him a bit. I think I can coax him over to my side."

"So you don't want me to follow him back to town?"

"There's no need," Waverly said. "Just go back to work."

"Yes, boss," Rogan said. "Whatever you say."

"And close the door," Waverly said. "I'll be sitting in here for a while."

"Sure, boss."

Rogan backed out, shutting the door behind him.

* * *

As PALMER LEFT the house, he saw one of the ranch hands holding his horse's reins by the corral. He walked over to claim the gelding.

"Pretty nice animal," the hand said. "What is he, five?"

"Exactly," Palmer said, taking the reins from the man.

"He's a healthy beast," the man said. "Nice deep chest. I'll bet he can run all day."

"I don't know yet," Palmer said. "I just got him."

He mounted the horse and looked down at the young ranch hand.

"Well, take my word for it," the young man said. "I know horses. This one can run."

"Then I'll test him and find out for myself," Palmer said. "Thanks."

"Sure thing, Marshal," the man said, "sure thing. I'll be seein' ya in town."

Palmer nodded, turned the horse, and rode away from the Bar W. He had formed his own opinion of Franklin Waverly. The man was used to getting his way. That meant Palmer would be hearing from him again in the very near future. It would be unavoidable.

PALMER GAVE THE gelding his head for a while, letting him run. He found out the kid at the ranch was right. Buddy could run all day long.

He brought the gelding back to the livery and handed him over to Lionel.

"You get along with 'im?" the old man asked.

"We got along great," Palmer said. "He can really run."

"Well, the mayor did tell me to take care of ya," Lionel said. "You'll let 'im know I did? You'll tell 'im?"

"Sure, I'll tell him," Palmer said. "Don't worry."

"Thanks, Marshal," the old man said. "I'll take good care of 'im for ya."

"Thanks, Lionel."

As Palmer started from the livery, Lionel called out to him.

"Didja get out to the Bar W okay?"

"I got there," Palmer said. He waved and left, heading for city hall.

H E PRESENTED HIMSELF to Mrs. McQueen, who took him in to see Mayor O'Connor.

"How's it going, Marshal?" the mayor asked. "Any problems?"

"Nope," Palmer said. "None, Mr. Mayor."

"What brings you here, then?"

"I just thought I'd tell you I had lunch with Franklin Waverly," Palmer said. "He invited me out to his place."

"Really? What did he want?"

"It's my opinion he was studying me, trying to decide if I could be bought."

"Bought?" O'Connor said. "Why would he— Oh, I see. You've heard stories about rich ranchers owning towns, along with the town lawmen."

"And politicians," Palmer added.

"You've been reading too many dime novels, Marshal. Waverly is good for this town. He doesn't want to own it."

"He backed your campaign, didn't he?"

"There!" O'Connor snapped. "Right there you can see he's not looking to own the town. He understood my promises to make this town grow, so he backed me. That's it."

"Are you sure?"

"Dead sure," O'Connor said. "I consider him our leading citizen."

"Well, okay, then," Palmer said. "I just wanted to get your take on him."

"I'm sure he just wanted to meet the new marshal," O'Connor went on.

"I'll take your word for it, Mr. Mayor," Palmer said. "Have a good day."

Palmer turned and left the mayor's office. Once outside, he became aware that Mrs. McQueen was staring at him.

"I'll bet you have all the answers to my questions," he said to her.

She didn't respond.

"But I don't suppose you'd give me any."

"Marshal," she said, "you're very new in town. I'm afraid you're going to have to earn any answers you get."

"Fair enough, ma'am," he said, and left the office and the building.

A FTER PALMER LEFT the city hall building, Mrs. McQueen went into the mayor's office.

"He has questions," she said.

"Did you answer them?"

"That's not my job," she said. "Besides, I told him he's going to have to earn whatever answers he gets."

"Well said, Mrs. McQueen."

"Is there anything I can do for you, sir?"

"No," Mayor O'Connor said, "you've done quite enough. Thank you."

"You're very welcome, sir," she said, and went back to her desk.

O'Connor wondered exactly what questions Marshal Cassidy had and how far the man would go to get his answers.

And he wondered if he had made the right choice in hiring him.

PALMER KNEW HE was going to have to make more of an effort to fit in. He didn't know how long he would be able to keep his job or even how long he'd want to. But for now this was the place for him, and he needed to blend in and not create any problems for himself. That meant handling the mayor, and Franklin Waverly, a little differently, maybe even giving them what they wanted, a pet lawman.

He had supper in his hotel dining room that night, again considering what kind of a lawman he should be, when suddenly Steve Atlee appeared in the doorway. He looked around the room, spotted Palmer, and came walking over.

"You mind if I sit, Marshal?"

"Is this about being a deputy again, Atlee?" Palmer asked.

"Not really," Atlee said. "But it might be about helpin' you."

"Have a seat," Palmer said, waving at the chair across from him. "You want something to eat or drink?"

Atlee looked at the half-finished steak on Palmer's plate and said, "Maybe coffee."

Palmer called the waiter over and said, "Bring my friend some coffee . . . and a steak."

"Yessir."

"Thanks, Marshal," Atlee said. "I am a bit hungry."

"I've got to tell you, Atlee," Palmer said, "I've been warned about you."

"By the mayor, I bet," Atlee said.

"That's right."

"There's a reason for that."

"And that would be?" Palmer asked.

"The sheriff and me, we wouldn't be the mayor's pet badge toters," Atlee said. "We upheld the law the way it was supposed to be, not the way O'Connor wanted us to. That's why we got fired and replaced by you."

Palmer studied the man, trying to decide if he was telling the truth.

"If that's true, what makes you think the mayor would let me pin a deputy's badge on you?"

"I kinda thought maybe you'd do it on your own," Atlee said.

"It's a little early in my job for me to push," Palmer said. "I'm still getting my bearings."

"That means you talked to Mr. Waverly?"

"How'd you know that?"

"I figured he'd wanna meet you," Atlee said. "Be-tween him and O'Connor, they figure they own everythin' around here. That includes that badge on your chest."

The waiter came with the coffee and the steak dinner.

"Why don't you tell me what you're doing here while you eat?" Palmer suggested.

Atlee picked up his knife and fork and attacked the steak ravenously.

"On second thought," Palmer said, "let's save that for dessert."

T HEY BOTH FINISHED their steak dinners, Atlee eating his entire meal in the time it took Palmer to eat what remained of his. After that, they had some more coffee with pie, and Palmer went back to their conversation.

"What's this about, Atlee?" he asked. "I know you didn't come here to bum a free meal."

"Marshal, I came here to warn you," Atlee said, "about the mayor and about Waverly. Neither of them is gonna back you, because they're too busy backin' each other."

"Tell me something," Palmer said. "Are they building this town up?"

"Well, yeah—"

"And isn't that what the mayor said he was going to do if he got elected?"

"I s'pose," Atlee said, "but I think you're gonna find out that people aren't too happy with some of the changes."

"That may be so," Palmer said. "But I was hired to do a job in this town."

"So go ahead and do it," Atlee said. "Just watch your back. Or hire a deputy who'll watch it for you."

"Meaning you?"

"I have experience," Atlee said. He stood up. "I live in town. You'll be able to find me when you're ready to hire me. Thanks for the meal, Marshal."

CHAPTER FOURTEEN

PALMER WAS LOOKING forward to his first Saturday night as marshal of Integrity. He had raised some hell in towns himself on Saturday night when he was younger, so he assumed there'd be some cowhands whooping it up in the saloons.

He started at the Palomino, where he had met Wade the bartender. As he walked in, everything looked and sounded more heightened than the first time he'd been there. The music was louder, as were the voices laughing and yelling, and the girls seemed to be moving about with more energy. The gaming tables looked like they were vibrating.

"Marshal," Wade said as Palmer approached the bar, "I been expectin' ya."

"I'll have a beer, Wade," Palmer said. "This place is really alive."

"I told you it would be," Wade said, setting a beer in front of him. "Have you checked the other places?"

"I did earlier in the week, but tonight I started here first."

"Well," Wade said, "we are the biggest and the best in town."

"Does that mean you have more trouble than the others?" Palmer asked, sipping his beer.

"Not at all," Wade said. "My customers come here to have a good time, not to start trouble."

"That's good to hear. I'll just watch while I drink my beer."

"Enjoy," Wade said, and moved on down the bar to serve other customers.

Palmer watched and listened, and although there were loud and gruff voices all around him, there was no indication of arguments brewing. He finished his beer and set the mug down.

"I like it," Palmer said. "I guess I'll move on and continue my rounds."

"Come on in anytime, Marshal," Wade said.

Palmer left the Palomino, feeling as if he hadn't made a ripple in the atmosphere there.

H E STOPPED NEXT at the Last Chance, where he'd met the bartender who said everybody just called him Bartender.

There were obvious differences between the Palomino and the Last Chance. Immediately as he entered, he heard voices raised in anger and had a feeling they were coming from a poker table.

He went to the bar, where a place opened for him as customers saw the badge. They actually moved away from him and eyed him suspiciously.

"There you are," Bartender said. "I figured you'd be comin' around tonight."

"Saturday night's the night, right?" Palmer asked.

"Yep. If you're lookin' for trouble, tonight's the night to find it, and this might be the place," Bartender said.

"Is that a poker game I hear?" Palmer asked.

"Yeah, there are some bad losers and bad players in the house tonight," Bartender said.

"Let me have a beer, Bartender," Palmer said, "and then I'll walk around and have a look."

"And let everybody have a look at you," Bartender said, setting a beer in front of him.

"Thanks."

Palmer carried his beer with him and started to stroll the room. The patrons stared at him curiously, moved aside, and watched as he made his way to the poker table where voices were still being raised.

"That's right," one voice said. "I'm callin' you a cheat."

"You ready to back that up, Wilkins?" another voice asked.

There were five men at the table. Of the two men arguing, one had stacks of chips in front of him, and the other—Wilkins—had almost none.

Calling a man a cheater in a game of poker usually provoked a violent response. That is, unless you could prove it.

"Yeah," Wilkins said, "I'm ready to back it up."

Palmer knew he had walked in just in time. As Wilkins started to stand and go for his gun, Palmer stepped in, grabbed his off arm, and turned him around.

"This is not a good idea," he said.

Wilkins was a hard-looking man in his forties. His mean eyes took Palmer in at a glance and then fixed on the badge on his chest.

"Ah, the new lawman in town," he said. "Tryin' to make your mark, Marshal, by gettin' in my business?"

Palmer looked at the other man, the big winner at the table. He was in his late thirties and wearing a gambler's suit and hat, all gray. Palmer was sure he had a gun under the jacket.

"Anybody else think this man's been cheating?" he asked.

The other three players at the table appeared to be local tradesmen.

"He ain't cheatin', Marshal," one of them said. "He's just damned good."

"And this fella?" Palmer asked, indicating Wilkins.

"Oh, he's just terrible," one of the other men said. "He never folds. Not ever."

"You can't win if you don't play," Wilkins said. "And this yahoo ain't that good. He's cheatin'."

"I'm afraid you're the only one who thinks so, Mr. Wilkins," Palmer said. "So I guess you'd better move along and let somebody else have your seat."

"You think you can make me move, Marshal?" Wilkins asked. "I ain't broken the law."

"Not yet," Palmer said. "I'm trying to keep from having to put you in a cell. I'm asking you to leave."

"Marshal," Wilkins said, "I'm gonna kill this sonofabitch, even if I have to kill you first. Nobody cheats me!"

"Mr. Wilkins," Palmer said, "I'm going to take my gun out of my holster, just so you can see it. I want you to look at it closely, and then I think you'll leave here." Palmer put his hand on his gun and saw the man tense. "I ain't going to use it. I'm just going to show it to you."

He drew his gun slowly with his right hand. He didn't grip the gun like he was going to use it, but just palmed it so he could show it to Wilkins. It had gotten very quiet in the saloon as everyone stopped what they were doing to watch the new lawman at work.

"See it?" he asked.

The gun sat on its side in his palm.

"What the hell are you talk—"

Palmer's hand suddenly darted forward, and his gun smashed into Wilkins' face. The man went down like he'd been poleaxed.

Suddenly, the room erupted into applause as Palmer slid his gun back into his holster.

"I'm going to need some volunteers to carry this man outside," Palmer announced.

Hurriedly, three men stepped forward.

"We takin' him to jail, Marshal?" one asked anxiously.

"No," Palmer said, "he's right. He hasn't broken the law yet. Just take him outside and lay him down on the ground."

"Yessir."

As the men lifted the unconscious Wilkins and carried him out, the gambler looked up at Palmer and said, "Much obliged, Marshal. I didn't want to have to kill him."

"And I didn't want you to kill him," Palmer said, "or him you, not on my first Saturday night on the job."

"Can't blame you for that."

"You gents go ahead and continue your game," Palmer said. "I'm sure you can get someone to fill the empty seat."

Palmer turned, walked to the bar, set his half-finished beer down, and handed Wilkins' gun to Bartender.

"Hang on to that for me, will ya?"

"Sure. That was somethin'," the man said.

"Thanks," Palmer said, and left the saloon.

T HEY HAD CARRIED Wilkins out and laid him in the street, just off the boardwalk. Palmer sat down next to him, removed his gun from his holster, and waited for him to come to.

"What the hell—" Wilkins sputtered as he woke. "You—you hit me in the face with your gun."

"I know," Palmer said, "not a smart thing to do. I could've bent the frame. But I think it's all right, and you're alive, so . . ."

Wilkins struggled to sit up, put his hand to his face. There was a knot on his forehead where Palmer's gun had struck him, and it was just starting to crack and bleed as it swelled larger.

"You're going to need to have that looked at, Wilkins," Palmer said.

Wilkins held his head in his hands for a moment, then looked at Palmer with mean eyes.

"Do you know who I am?" he demanded.

"Hmm, let me guess," Palmer said. "Jesse James? Billy the Kid? Am I getting close?"

"This ain't funny!" Wilkins snapped.

"It would've been even less funny if you'd ended up dead," Palmer said.

"I could've taken that gambler," Wilkins told him.

"Sure, you would've killed him, and then I would've had to kill you. This way everybody stayed alive."

"And what do you expect me to do now?"

"Move on," Palmer said. "Go home, get some sleep, sober up, and have that looked at in the morning. There is a doctor in this town, isn't there?"

Wilkins nodded and said, "Doc Stack."

"Well, go and see him in the morning, Wilkins," Palmer said.

Wilkins put his hand down to his holster.

"Where's my gun?"

"I have it," Palmer said. "You'll get it back tomorrow, after you see the doc. Come to my office."

Wilkins started to get to his feet, but needed help from Palmer to do so. When he was up, he staggered for a moment.

"Can you walk?" Palmer asked.

"I'll walk."

"Good," Palmer said. "Walk home, Wilkins. I'll see you in the morning in my office after you see the doc."

Wilkins put his hand to his head, then looked at the blood on his palm.

"That was a dirty trick," he said, and started walking away.

PALMER WENT BACK into the saloon and up to the bar.

"I'll take that gun," he told Bartender.

The man handed it to him and he slid it into his belt.

"That was pretty slick," Bartender said. "Where'd you learn that trick?"

"I saw Bill Hickok do it once."

"Is that for real?"

Palmer nodded. What he didn't tell the man was that Wild Bill had done it to him when he was younger, rather than kill him.

"It's for real," he said.

"I thought Hickok was a killer," Bartender said.

"When he had to be," Palmer said. He looked around, then glanced at the batwing doors. Apparently, Wilkins was not coming back in.

"Nice crowd," he said, preparing to leave.

"Where are you headed?" Bartender asked.

"The Little Dakota."

"Ah," Bartender said, "if you think this was trouble, wait until you get there."

CHAPTER FIFTEEN

H E'D BEEN WARNED several times that the Little
Dakota was rough, especially on Saturday night,
but when he got there, the place was as quiet as a
church, even though most of the tables seemed occu-
pied. There was room at the bar, though, where only a
few men were lounging.

He walked to the bar, and although heads didn't
turn, he felt the eyes on him—including those of the
old bartender whose name he never got the first time
he was there.

"Marshal," the old man said, "you havin' a drink
while you're here?"

"No," Palmer said, "I doubt there's a clean glass in
the house. No offense."

"Offense taken," the old man said. "Whataya want,
then?"

"Just taking a look at the place on Saturday night," Palmer said.

"This is as rowdy as you're gonna see it in here," the bartender said.

"That's not what I heard," Palmer said, looking around.

"This is my regular crowd, Marshal," the man said. "It's when a stranger—like you—comes in that somethin' might happen."

"I didn't get your name last time I was here," Palmer said.

"My name's Art Pope. The folks hereabouts just call me Artie."

"Well, Artie," Palmer said, "I've got to tell you I'm feeling like somebody's trying to pull the wool over my eyes. This is my first Saturday on the job, and I figure you were expecting me."

"Don't know what yer talkin' about, Marshal," Artie said. "This is just a nice, quiet place."

Palmer looked around again, saw several heads duck away as he did. He was sure the word had gone out that when the new marshal walked in, everybody was supposed to keep their heads down and their mouths shut. Well, it wouldn't be a bad thing if they all behaved every time he came around.

"Sure you don't want a drink?" Artie asked.

"I'm sure, Artie," Palmer said, looking down at the grime that covered the bar. "You really should clean this place up sometime."

"Sure thing, Marshal," Artie said, "I'll get right on that. Come back anytime."

Palmer looked around one more time before turning and heading for the door.

* * *

THE SILVER SPUR was Palmer's next stop. The music, chips, and laughter he'd heard his first visit seemed even louder this time.

The bartender Skinny watched as Palmer approached the bar. He leaned forward and said something, and several men moved to accommodate the new marshal.

"Skinny," Palmer said.

"Evenin', Marshal," Skinny said. "You should know Brazos and his friends are in the back."

"That's okay," Palmer said. "I'm just here to have a look around. Not to make trouble."

"Well, if you stay around here long enough," Skinny said, "it's gonna find you."

"I'm just finishing up my rounds, Skinny," Palmer said, "so if there's trouble, I'll be in my office. If it finds me there, I'll be ready."

"I'll keep that in mind, Marshal," Skinny said. "You want a drink before you go?"

"No, thanks," Palmer said. "I'm about five minutes away from a cup of coffee."

Palmer touched the brim of his hat and left, heading for his office.

HIS FIRST SATURDAY night had been uneventful, which suited him just fine. Sunday morning he was in his office after having breakfast in his hotel. He saw people in the dining room who were dressed for church. He didn't know if the real Abe Cassidy had been a religious man or not, but he certainly wasn't.

When the mayor entered his office wearing a black Sunday suit, he figured he was going to have some explaining to do.

"Marshal," Mayor O'Connor said, "ready for church?"

"Not today, Mr. Mayor," Palmer said, "and probably not ever."

"Really?" O'Connor said. "In your letters you came off as a very religious man. I thought for sure you'd want to go to church your first Sunday here. We have a couple of different denominations in town."

"That's all right," Palmer said. "You just go on ahead without me."

"I suppose I can't blame you," O'Connor said then. "You must be pretty angry with the Lord for what happened to your family."

"Please don't try to tell me that He moves in mysterious ways," Palmer said, "or that He has a plan. There's no plan that calls for children to be killed."

"Well," O'Connor said, "if you change your mind in the future, I know my church would be happy to have you."

"I thank you for the invitation," Palmer said.

"To each his own, Marshal," O'Connor said. "You have a nice morning."

Palmer sat back in his chair as the mayor left his office. It sure felt like the man had given him a way out even before he'd thought of it himself. He had managed to read all the letters the real Cassidy had received from the mayor. He only wished he could see the letters Cassidy had sent. He wondered what else there was about the man he didn't know that he was going to have to fake.

* * *

PALMER GOT OUT of the office and walked around, seeing a slight difference in the town on Sunday morning. Many of the businesses were not open yet, as the owners were probably in their chosen houses of worship. People were walking the street, heading to church and eyeing their new lawman. He knew some were wondering why he wasn't in church. Others probably didn't care.

The saloons weren't open for business, but when he looked in the window of the Palomino, he saw Wade behind the bar, wiping it down. The bartender looked up, as if he sensed he was being watched, waved at Palmer, and came to the door.

"Marshal," he said, "you wanna come in for coffee?"

"Why not?" Palmer said.

Palmer entered and followed Wade to the bar. The man poured him a cup of coffee and pushed it over to him.

"Why aren't you in church?" Palmer asked.

"I don't worship," Wade said. "At least, not any kind of God."

"You don't believe in God?"

"Lemme just say if there is a God, He's got a lot of explainin' to do." Wade studied Palmer for a moment. "You must feel the same way after what happened to your family."

"I do," Palmer said. "I told the mayor as much this morning when he came to take me to church."

"Oh, yeah," Wade said, "our mayor is a devout Catholic."

Palmer sipped from his cup.

"Good coffee," he said. "You don't serve this to your customers, do you?"

"Nope, I just make it for myself," Wade said, "and occasionally a friend who comes around."

"How many of those friends do you have?"

"So far," Wade said, "just you."

"Are we friends?" Palmer asked.

"We're gettin' there," Wade said. "How was your Saturday night?"

"Quiet."

"Do you wonder why that was?"

"I figure word got around the new lawman was on duty, so everybody was on their best behavior."

"You got it," Wade said. "Skinny and Artie put the word out."

"Not you?"

"Hey," Wade said, pouring more coffee for both of them, "I leave my customers on their own. They want to tangle with you, that's up to them."

"You got a shotgun under the bar?" Palmer asked.

"Oh, yeah, and a pretty good-sized club."

"I figured."

"I tend to handle rowdy customers myself," Wade explained, "but if it comes to gunplay, well, I'll probably leave that to you."

"Much obliged," Palmer said sarcastically.

"So you stuck your head inside all the saloons last night?" Wade said. "How about all the churches Sunday morning?"

"No churches for me," Palmer said.

"Guess I can't blame you for feeling that way," Wade said.

"Folks on the street were looking at me kind of funny this morning, but I've got to go with my feelings."

"You want me to sweeten your coffee a bit?" Wade asked, producing a bottle of whiskey.

"Why not?" Palmer said, pushing his cup closer to Wade.

CHAPTER SIXTEEN

MARSHAL ABRAHAM CASSIDY—Palmer had started to think of himself by that name—stepped out of his hotel and took a deep breath of crisp morning air into his lungs. It was getting colder as winter approached, but Palmer was finding he liked the weather, even though he had spent most of his life in the arid Southwest. He had bought himself some heavier shirts and a couple of jackets from the mercantile store, all at the suggestion of Belle Henderson. Palmer had taken to doing his shopping when Belle was around and her husband wasn't. She continued to flirt with him, but neither of them had tried to take the flirtation any further.

Two months into his tenure as town marshal, Palmer had used his jail cells on only three occasions, and all those were rowdy, sloppy drunks. One was from the Palomino Saloon, the other two from the Last Chance.

The patrons of the Little Dakota had continued to be on their best behavior, but he knew that wouldn't go on forever.

He'd had breakfast in the hotel, as he usually did. It was just more convenient. The same was true of having his supper each night at the Sweetwater. The owners of both eateries were committed to feeding him for free. Palmer finally accepted, figuring it was part of his salary and not a handout—like his hotel room.

He had gotten into the habit of walking around town after breakfast, just watching it wake up. Storekeepers were unlocking their doors, sweeping the boardwalk in front of their places, just opening for business. Most of them had gotten into the habit of waving or even calling out, "Mornin', Marshal." They were beginning to accept him.

He finished his walk at his office, did his own bit of sweeping out front and inside. He locked up when he went to his hotel for the night. The only time he stayed in the office overnight was when he had somebody in a cell. Up to this point, he hadn't seen the need for any deputies, although Steve Atlee still dropped in from time to time to check.

Palmer was starting to feel comfortable in his new identity. He kept his face clean-shaven, and his hair cut short, so that he looked little or nothing like Tom Palmer the outlaw. If anyone who had known him slightly ever came to town, they wouldn't recognize him. He checked the new wanted posters when they came out, but there were none of Tom Palmer because he wasn't wanted in South Dakota. How could he be? He'd never been there until coming to Integrity to take this job.

He was feeling very comfortable inside Abe Cassidy's skin. He had even made a couple of friends in Wade, the bartender at the Palomino, and Belle Henderson—if you could call a man whose last name he didn't know and a married woman his friends.

He stayed out of the saloons except for an occasional beer and his rounds. Sometimes he'd stop at the Palomino before it opened to have coffee with Wade. He did no gambling, didn't dally with any of the girls, didn't even play checkers with anyone. He simply didn't want to get that close to people.

He did his job the best way he knew how. So far, there had been no complaints from the mayor, and no run-ins with Franklin Waverly or any of the hands from his ranch. Occasionally, he saw Rogan in town, and they exchanged only nods. So far, neither Waverly nor the mayor had made any attempts to buy his badge. Maybe he'd managed to convince them it wasn't possible. He was pretty sure he'd convinced himself. So far, he was happy with the time he had spent on this side of the tin star.

Was he lonely? Not really. Even as the outlaw Tom Palmer, he had never really had close friends. In the outlaw life, there was too much chance a friend would turn on you. Money did that to people. So far, in the life of a lawman, he hadn't had to worry about any of those things. He hadn't even taken his gun from his holster, except for that one time with Wilkins—who seemed to be making sure their paths didn't cross again.

On this day he relaxed at his desk with a cup of coffee, ready for another quiet day.

But all good things had to come to an end. . . .

* * *

THE NOISE DREW Palmer out of his office on the run.
They were the first shots he had heard since arriv-
ing in Integrity. He saw several men running past his
office, didn't know if they were running toward the
shooting, or away from it, until he heard another shot.
He fell into step behind them.

Dust was being kicked up in the street as a group of
men on horseback was riding away. At first Palmer
thought it was a bank robbery, but then he realized the
activity had not taken place at the bank, but at the
mercantile store.

There was a crowd just outside the door. He pushed
his way through and entered. There were already some
people inside.

"Out of the way, move away!" he yelled. "What's
going on?"

People stepped aside and Palmer approached the
front counter. A man was sprawled across it, blood
pooling beneath his body. All around him the store
was a shambles, as if a violent fight had taken place.

"It's Henderson," somebody said, "the owner."

"They shot 'im!" another yelled.

Palmer leaned over the body, moved it just enough
to determine that the man was dead, having been shot
several times. Then he heard a moan from behind the
counter. He leaned over and saw Belle Henderson lying on the floor, bleeding but alive.

"Somebody get the doctor!" he yelled. "Now!"

One man separated himself from the group and ran
out of the store.

Palmer hurried around the counter and knelt down next to Belle.

"Belle? Can you hear me?"

She was lying on her back, staring up at the ceiling. At the sound of his voice, her eyes flickered.

"Abraham?" she said.

"Take it easy."

He saw the blood pulsing from a wound near her abdomen. He looked around, spotted a towel, wadded it up, and pressed it to the wound to try to stop the bleeding.

"You're going to be all right," he told her. "You're going to be fine."

"It . . . it hurts," she said. "Where-where's Ken?"

"Don't worry about Ken," Palmer said. "Just hang on. The doc's coming."

She reached out her hand and he took it. Her grip was very tight.

"That's it," he said. "Just keep squeezing my hand." He looked up. "Where's the damn doctor?"

"Here!" someone yelled, and then he appeared. "Excuse me, pardon me. Marshal, please move!"

Palmer knew the doctor's name was Stack, but he had not had an opportunity to meet him before this.

He released Belle's hand and withdrew from behind the counter so the doctor could get in.

"Who saw what happened?" he called out. "Anyone?"

"Marshal!" somebody called. Others moved aside so the spokesman could step forward. He was a young man, probably not yet twenty.

"I didn't see what happened, but I heard the shots and then saw four men come running out," he said.

"There was a fifth man outside holding all their horses."

It sounded like a setup for a bank robbery, only the mercantile store was nowhere near the bank.

"Did you know any of the men?" Palmer asked.

"No, sir, never saw 'em before."

"All right, put the word out," Palmer said. "I need a posse. Any volunteers can meet me out front with their horses. Go!"

"Yessir!"

"And go to the livery stable and tell Lionel to saddle my horse and bring it over."

"Yessir!"

The young man turned and left.

"Marshal," Doc Stack said, "get these people out of here. And I'll need two men to carry Mrs. Henderson to my office."

"You heard him," Palmer said. "Everybody out, except you and you." He pointed at two men. Then he turned to the doctor. "Is she going to make it?"

"I don't know. You slowed the bleeding with that towel, but I have to move her to my surgery and get that bullet out. Excuse me."

He instructed the two men on how to carry the injured woman, and they left the store, heading for his office. But before going the doctor turned and spoke to Palmer again.

"You'd better have somebody take Mr. Henderson over to the undertaker."

"Right. You heard him." He pointed at two of the remaining stragglers. "You and you, carry him over there."

Palmer knew he had two choices: ride out immediately with a posse to track the gunmen, or wait and see if Belle could tell him anything helpful about them. Actually, the decision was being made for him before he even came out. The crowd had dispersed; his horse was there, standing alone. There were no volunteers for a posse.

Except one.

Steve Atlee was waiting, holding his horse's reins.

"I'm ready, Marshal," he said.

"This is it?" Palmer asked.

"You ain't gonna get nobody else in this town to volunteer," Atlee told him.

"We've got at least five men to track, Atlee," Palmer said.

"You and me, we can handle 'em," Atlee said.

Palmer stood there, unclear about his next move. Should they mount up and ride after the men? The longer he waited to make a decision, the farther away they would get. He had been on the other side of a posse many times. He knew that sometimes they began the chase immediately. Other times it took a while to assemble enough men, and then they tracked rather than chased.

"Atlee, I've got to check on Belle—Mrs. Henderson," Palmer said. "I want to see if she can tell us what happened or who those men were. While I do that, you go and look for more volunteers."

"You ain't gonna get any, Marshal."

"Go talk to Wade at the Palomino," Palmer said. "See if he'll come and if he can suggest anybody. Meet me at the doc's office."

"Well, okay, but—"

"Just do it!" Palmer snapped. "I'm deputizing you."

"All right!" Atlee said, almost with glee.

Palmer grabbed his horse's reins and walked the animal over to Doc Stack's office.

There were people gathered out front when he got there.

"You people go home," he said. "If any of you men want to join the posse, get your horse and meet me back here. Now go!"

He could tell from their faces, none of them was going to volunteer.

He tied his horse off and went inside. One man was standing there, apparently worried. He looked like a faded fifty-five or so and was wearing a white apron.

"Who are you?" Palmer asked.

"My name's Ralph Waters," he said. "The Hendersons are our friends. My wife is in there helpin' the doc. Is Ken dead, Marshal?"

"Yes, he is."

"Damn it."

"Did you see or hear anything?"

"No," Waters said. "We have the hardware store down the street. We heard the shots and came runnin' out just in time to see the men ride off."

"Recognize any of them?"

"No, not a one."

"Did you see their faces?"

"One or two."

"Could you point them out if you saw them again?"

"Gee, I don't know. . . ."

"How is she?" Palmer asked.

"I don't know," he said. "My wife, Reba, sometimes acts as a nurse for the doc, so we came over to see if we could help."

"I'm sure Belle—Mrs. Henderson will appreciate that," Palmer said.

"Are you gettin' a posse together, Marshal?"

"I'm trying, but so far with no success."

"Well, I'll go," Waters said. "I ain't a good rider, and the only shootin' I done is huntin' rabbits, but—"

"Relax, Mr. Waters," Palmer said. "I'll be needing more experienced men than you." *And younger and fitter,* he added to himself.

"Right, right," the man said.

The doctor came out of his surgery. He had a long white apron on, and it was covered with fresh blood.

"Good, you're here," he said. "She wants to talk to you."

"Is she all right, Doc?" Palmer asked. "Is she going to make it?"

"It's still touch and go," the sawbones said. "I got the bullet out. That's half the battle. The other half is up to her. Now, don't make her talk long. I need her to rest."

"Right . . ."

Palmer entered the room, saw Belle lying on an examination table with a fiftyish woman sitting next to her, holding her hand.

"The marshal's here, Belle," the woman said, and moved out of the way. She touched Palmer's arm as she went by, as if trying to soothe him.

Palmer walked to the table. Belle looked pale and small. He took her hand.

"I'm here, Belle."

For a moment he thought she was unconscious, but then her eyes fluttered open. She looked at him and held his hand tight.

"One of them . . ." she said. "One of them called another one . . . Teach."

"Teach?" Palmer said. "Was that his name?"

She wet her lips and said, "He got—got real angry and . . . and hit the other man in the face. His mouth . . . was bloody."

One man was called Teach, and another had a bloody mouth.

"Can you tell me anything else, Belle?" he asked. "Did you know who they were?"

"One man . . . one man had been in the store before . . . talkin' to Ken. I asked him . . . asked him what . . . what it was about and Ken . . . Ken told me to . . . to mind my business."

"So your husband knew these men," Palmer said. "Was he doing some kind of business with them? Belle?"

Her eyes closed and her grip weakened.

"That's it," Doc said, coming up behind him. "She needs to rest. You get out and do your job. Leave me to do mine."

"Right," Palmer said. "Right you are, Doc."

On his way out he stopped to look at the Waters couple.

"You folks keep helping," he said.

"We will, Marshal," the woman said. "You get those bastards!"

"I plan to, Mrs. Waters," Palmer said. "I plan to."

CHAPTER SEVENTEEN

WHEN PALMER CAME out of the doctor's office he found Atlee waiting with Wade, the bartender from the Palomino. Both men were mounted and holding rifles.

"Nobody else?" he asked.

"This is the best you're gonna get, Abe," Wade said to him.

Palmer mounted his gelding.

"I appreciate this, Wade," he said.

"Hey, I like both Ken and Belle," Wade said. "Is she all right?"

"Doc got the bullet out. The rest is up to her."

"She tell you anythin'?" Atlee asked.

"A little bit," Palmer said. "I'll fill you in on the way. Let's not let them get too far ahead of us."

"I grabbed some coffee and beef jerky, just in case we're out there overnight," Wade said.

"Good man," Palmer said. He should have thought of that himself. "Let's go. There're five of them, so their trail shouldn't be too hard to follow. By the way," he added to Wade, "you're deputized, too."

THE MAIN ROAD into Integrity had a lot of tracks made by horses and wagon wheels. They had to wait until they got outside of town to pick out the tracks they wanted.

"Five horses riding together," Palmer said from one knee. He stood up and mounted his horse.

"How good are you at reading sign?" Wade asked.

"Good enough to follow these killers," Palmer assured him.

"What about you, Steve?" Wade asked.

"Just enough to know they're ridin' hell-bent for leather."

"Do we have any idea what they were doin' in town?" Wade asked. "Were they robbin' the store, or were they there specifically to kill Ken, for some reason?"

"We don't know," Palmer said. "Belle says she saw one of the men with her husband before. That means Ken knew at least one of them."

As they started riding again, Wade asked, "Why would anybody wanna kill Ken Henderson? He was a storekeeper."

"Who knows?" Palmer said.

"And why shoot Belle?"

"Probably because she was a witness," Palmer said. "Or maybe she got hit by a stray shot."

"Hey," Atlee said, "anybody fire shots at these yahoos while they was ridin' out? Maybe one of them is hurt."

"I don't recall any shots once they got mounted and started riding away," Palmer said. "I think all the shots came from inside the store."

"This musta been personal," Wade said. "I mean, why rob a mercantile when you could rob a bank?"

"Maybe the bank was too hard," Atlee said.

"Are you kidding?" Palmer said. "That place is a cracker box."

He had decided long ago that the bank would be easy to take, if he decided to hit the outlaw trail again. The only thing wrong with it was that it never had a lot of money in it. Even Franklin Waverly never kept his Bar W payroll there.

On the other hand, Palmer knew when Waverly brought his payroll in by armored wagon to his ranch house. Hitting that would have been worth it. But that didn't happen this time of the month. No, Wade was probably right. This was personal. The killers had something against Ken Henderson, and they had ridden into town to kill him. Belle just happened to get caught in whatever shenanigans her husband was involved with.

The trail being left by the five horses was taking them southwest, which was a direction Palmer didn't want to go in. The last thing he wanted to do was leave South Dakota, but these were killers he was tracking. He knew posses to give up chasing bank robbers after a while, but he also knew of those that followed killers into Mexico if they had to.

As the sun got high in the sky at midday, Wade asked, "How far are we gonna trail 'em?"

"As far as it takes," Palmer said. "This is the first bit of trouble we've had since I put the badge on. I've got to show that this is not something anybody can get away with in Integrity."

"What if they cross into Nebraska or Wyoming?" Wade asked. "Or even Montana? You've got no jurisdiction in those territories."

"Murder is murder, Wade," Palmer said. "If they cross a border, so will I. Neither of you has to come with me."

"You ain't gonna track five men alone, Marshal," Atlee said. "I'm with ya."

Wade hesitated, and Palmer gave him his out.

"You've got a business to run, Wade," he said. He knew Wade actually owned the Palomino and didn't just tend bar. "You can head back anytime."

"We're not at that point yet, Abe," Wade said.

"Just so you know," Palmer said. "I don't expect you to ignore your business."

"I appreciate that, Abe," Wade said.

Atlee grabbed his canteen, but shook it and decided against a drink.

"We're gonna need some water," he said. "I think there's a water hole up ahead."

"You know this area?" Palmer asked.

"Some," Atlee said. "That's why I'm sayin' I think there's a water hole up ahead. I woulda known more if they'd gone north."

"Maybe they stopped for water, too," Wade said.

"I hope so," Palmer said. "It'd give me a chance to read their sign while they're standing still. I want to see their boot prints as well as their hoofprints."

"They're gonna have to camp for the night, Marshal," Atlee said. "If we keep ridin', we should catch up to 'em."

Maybe Atlee did have some of the experience he claimed to have.

"At night?" Wade asked. "One of our horses steps in a chuckhole and we're ruined."

"We wouldn't even hafta push," Atlee went on. "We just need to keep movin' while they're standin' still. If we go slow, we'll avoid chuckholes."

Wade looked at Palmer, who said, "He has a point."

"It'll be up to you," Wade said.

"Yeah, it will," Palmer said.

I T TURNED OUT Atlee was right about the water hole. They were able to water the horses, fill their canteens, and study tracks left by the killers they were trailing.

"Most of these boots have run-down heels," Palmer said. "Should be easy to identify."

"I see somethin' here, Marshal," Atlee said, crouched down and pointing.

Palmer walked over with Wade behind him.

"What is it?" the bartender asked.

Palmer looked over Atlee's shoulder.

"Looks like a horse has gone lame," he said.

"You can tell that from the tracks?" Wade asked.

Palmer pointed.

"The horse is favoring his left front," he said. "That's going to slow them down."

"Or just the rider," Atlee said, "if they leave him behind."

"As we go along we should be able to tell if he's still

with them," Palmer said. "If they leave him and we catch up to him, he can tell us who the rest are. When we have names, we can put the word out."

"And head back to town?" Wade asked.

"Yes," Palmer said. "With a prisoner we'd go back to town and get the whole story out of him."

Atlee looked up.

"We still have a few hours of daylight," he said.

"He's right," Palmer said. "Let's move."

A S IT CAME on dusk, Palmer and Atlee decided that the lame horse had been left behind.

"He's either walking it or riding double with somebody," Palmer said. "Could be we'll just catch up to the horse."

"Still," Atlee said, "even ridin' double is gonna slow somebody down."

It was getting cold as darkness fell. Normally, they would have camped and built a fire. It was up for discussion.

"There's not gonna be much of a moon tonight," Wade said, making the best point.

"He's right," Palmer said. "Let's camp, and come morning we can start moving faster. We're sure to catch up to that lame horse. One way or another, we might learn something."

"Marshal," Atlee said, "you mind if I scout up ahead a bit in the dark? I might spot a campfire."

"Good point, Steve," Palmer said, "but don't go too far."

As Atlee rode on, Palmer built a fire while Wade

took care of the horses. Soon, they were seated around the campfire with coffee and beef jerky.

"I'm thinking Atlee's been telling me the truth all this time," Palmer said. "He does seem to be pretty experienced as a deputy. I wonder why Mayor O'Connor warned me off him."

"I'm gonna say he has experience," Wade said, "but he can also be a loose cannon. He does seem to be happy to follow you, though."

"He's been making some good suggestions," Palmer said. "I think when we get back I'll argue his case to the mayor."

"So you're gonna take 'im on full-time as a deputy?" Wade asked.

"Judging from what I've seen so far, yes," Palmer said. "Unless, like you say, he shows his loose-cannon side."

"Well," Wade said, "there's time enough for anythin' to happen."

THEY HEARD A horse approaching, picked up their rifles until they saw Atlee riding into camp.

"I'll take your horse," Wade said as the man dismounted.

"Thanks."

As he walked to the fire, Palmer handed him a cup of coffee.

"See anything?" he asked.

"No," Atlee said. "I went as far as I dared, but Wade was right. Without the moonlight it's too dangerous."

Palmer handed him a piece of beef jerky. Wade returned to the fire.

"We'd better set watches, just to be on the safe side," Palmer said.

"I'll go first," Atlee said.

"Then me," Wade said.

"We'll get an early start, at first light," Palmer said. "Some coffee to warm our bellies, and then we'll go."

Palmer and Wade turned in while Atlee stoked the fire and made another pot of coffee.

A S THE SUN started to come up, Palmer killed the fire and poured the last of the coffee. He woke each man and handed him a cup.

"Time to go," he said.

Wade drank his coffee and said, "I'll saddle the horses."

"I'll pack the saddlebags," Atlee said.

Palmer made sure the fire was out, kicked and scattered the remnants. Then they all mounted up and headed out.

CHAPTER EIGHTEEN

T HEY RODE AT a quick pace. Occasionally, Atlee would move ahead of them to scout. In the afternoon, he came riding back in a hurry.

"Hey, hey," he called out. "I found it."

"Found what?" Wade asked.

"The lame horse," Atlee said. "I mean, I saw it up ahead. We can catch up to it easy."

"Lead the way."

They followed Atlee at a run and soon saw the lame horse up ahead. They slowed so as not to spook it.

"Wait here," Palmer said, dismounting.

He walked toward the horse, who was skittish but didn't try to run. He spoke to it softly as he approached, and finally was able to grab the reins and stroke the horse's nose.

"Come on," he called. "I got him."

Wade and Atlee led their horses and Palmer's until they reached him and the loose horse.

"Let's check the saddlebags," Palmer said, "see if there's anything there that can tell us something."

Wade stepped up to hold the horse's reins while Palmer went through the saddlebags.

"Nothing," he said when he was done.

Atlee had been walking the area, searching the ground, and now he called out, "Look here."

Palmer walked over.

"What is it?" Wade asked.

"Boot prints," Palmer said. "This fella's on foot. The others left him behind."

"Then he can't be far ahead," Wade said.

"Leave the horse," Palmer said. "Let's ride."

U P AHEAD, THEY found two cold campsites. The first had been made by one man, who'd kept warm with a small fire. The next one, a few miles away, was larger; four men had picketed their horses, made a fire, and spent the night.

"They didn't go much farther after leavin' him," Atlee observed.

"Yeah, but they've put some miles between them today," Palmer said. "I'm thinking they left him behind for more reasons than a lame horse."

"And that would be?" Wade asked.

"To keep us busy," Palmer said. "They figure we'll take the time to question him, maybe even take him back to town before we do."

"Which is exactly what we were thinkin' o' doin'," Atlee said.

"Right," Palmer said.

"So what *will* we do when we catch up to him?" Wade asked.

"Convince him that his best bet is to tell us who the others are and where they're going," Palmer said.

"By doin' what?" Wade asked. "Promisin' to let him go?"

"No," Palmer said. "By promisin' to keep him alive."

W HEN THEY SPOTTED him up ahead, he was limping along, carrying a canteen. He heard their horses behind him and turned to see who it was. He was smart enough to drop the canteen and put his hands high in the air.

"Just stand easy," Palmer said when they caught up to him.

"I ain't gonna try nothin'," the man said. "Those bastards left me behind."

Palmer, Atlee, and Wade dismounted. Wade held their horses while Palmer and Atlee approached the man. Palmer plucked the outlaw's gun from his holster and tossed it aside.

"Okay, put your hands down," he said. "I'm Marshal Cassidy from Integrity."

"I figured," the man said. "The name's Pike."

"Well, Mr. Pike," Palmer said, "you've got two choices. Tell us about what happened in town, or we'll take your boots and socks and leave you on foot."

"You don't gotta threaten me, Marshal," Pike said. "Them bastards left me behind with nothin' but a canteen, which is empty now."

Palmer looked over at Wade, who took one of their

canteens and tossed it to him. Palmer caught it and
gave it to Pike. He drank thirstily and handed it back.

"Thanks, Marshal."

"Who killed Ken Henderson, Pike?" Palmer asked.

Of course, if Pike had killed him, he was going to
try to lay the blame on one of the others. But if he was
the killer, Palmer doubted Pike would be the one the
others left behind like this. They were tossing him to
the wolves to give themselves more time to get away.

"That was all Dancy," Pike said. "I just stayed outside holding the horses."

"Why'd this Dancy kill him?" Palmer asked.

"I dunno, I swear. He just said it was somethin' personal," Pike said.

"What's this fella's full name?" Palmer asked.

"Jack Dancy," Pike said.

"I never heard of him," Palmer said. He looked at
Atlee. "You?"

"Yeah," Atlee said, "him and his gang usually go
after banks, not mercantile stores. So I guess this
musta been personal, like this fella says."

Palmer directed himself back to Pike.

"What's he look like?"

"Mean and ugly," Pike said. "He's a big man with a
scar here." He drew his fingers down his face.

Palmer looked at Atlee.

"That sound right?"

"Yeah, I heard about the scar."

"Is there a town near here, Steve?" Palmer asked.

"Geez, I dunno, Marshal."

"There is," Pike said.

They looked at him.

"It's called Kennerville," Pike told them. "That's where I was headed. I didn't think I could make it anywhere else on foot."

"What's there?" Palmer asked.

"Not much."

"Law?"

"I don't think so."

"Telegraph?"

Pike shook his head.

"Not a chance."

"How far is it?"

"It's a few miles yet. I was hopin' to get there before dark."

"I guess that'll depend on how fast you can walk," Palmer said.

"What?"

"Where are Dancy and the others headed, Pike?" Palmer asked.

Still frowning Pike said, "They wasn't gonna stop until they got to Wyoming."

"Where in Wyoming?" Palmer asked.

"Most likely Sheridan," Pike said. "Dancy's got a woman there. Works in a joint called the Buffalo Saloon. Her name's Lily. He talks about her all the time."

"Wade," Palmer said, "you take Mr. Pike here to Kennerville. Get him a horse and then bring him back to Integrity and put him in a cell."

"I thought maybe you'd let me go after I helped ya," Pike said.

"We'll see if everything you've told us is true, Pike," Palmer said. "Meanwhile, you'll sit in a cell." Palmer looked at Atlee. "Tie his hands behind him."

"Yessir."

Palmer walked to Wade.

"You sure you want me to go back?" Wade asked.

"Positive," Palmer said. "Atlee and me, we're going to head for Sheridan."

"You believe 'im?" Wade asked.

"I do," Palmer said. "I don't think he's happy about being left behind. You take him back, put him in a cell. Deputize somebody you trust to sit on him and feed him till we get back."

"And what do I tell people?"

"Just that he was one of the five men, nothing more," Palmer said. "Tell them me and Atlee will be bringing in the other four."

"All right, Abe," Wade said. "Whatever you say."

He took his horse's reins from Wade. Atlee came over and did the same. The two of them mounted up as Wade walked over to Pike.

"He gives you any trouble," Palmer said, "shoot him."

"I ain't gonna be no trouble," Pike said.

"See to it you ain't," Palmer said. "Wade here is one of my best men, and he's not going to take any guff from the likes of you."

Wade looked like what he was, a rather mild-mannered bartender, but because Wade was the owner of the Palomino, Palmer knew he had more backbone than that. Wade gave Pike a mean look that was meant to convey that to him.

As Palmer and Atlee turned their horses and rode off, Wade picked up Pike's discarded gun and stuck it in his belt.

"Is he gonna be all right?" Atlee asked as they rode away.

"He'll be fine," Palmer said. "All he's got to do is take Pike back and stick him in a cell. Let's you and me head for Sheridan and find Lily."

CHAPTER NINETEEN

THEY PUSHED THEIR horses to the limit and made it to Sheridan in two days.

"Should we check in with the local law?" Atlee asked.

"Let's find the Buffalo Saloon first," Palmer said.

He was slightly nervous about being in Sheridan. He'd been there once before, not for very long and with a full beard. There was always a chance somebody would recognize him, but it was a small chance. Besides, the town had grown by leaps and bounds and was much bigger now. And Atlee and he weren't going to be there very long.

They found the Buffalo and dismounted.

"We goin' in?" Atlee asked.

Palmer took off his badge, put it in his shirt pocket,

and said, "We are. Just follow my lead and don't do anything until I say."

"Gotcha, Marshal."

The loud music and voices poured out over the batwing doors. Palmer and Atlee entered and headed straight for the bar, which was the longest Palmer had ever seen. He didn't think the Buffalo had been there the one time he'd been to town.

"Two beers," Palmer told the bartender.

"Wow, this place is lively," Atlee said, "and it looks like they got half a dozen girls workin' the floor. I wonder which one's Lily."

"We may just have to ask," Palmer said, handing Atlee his beer, "but let's start by watching for a man with a scar."

"Do you think it's possible we beat them here?" Atlee asked.

"Not judging from the tracks we saw," Palmer said. Even though Sheridan's streets were covered by tracks left by horses and wagons, Palmer was pretty sure the four killers had reached Sheridan first. The question was, were they still there?

"So we're just gonna wait for them to come in?" Atlee asked.

"No, we can't do that," Palmer said. "They may have been here and gone already. No, we're going to have to talk to Lily."

"So how do we find her?"

"Like I said before," Palmer answered, "we ask."

They turned back to the bar and Palmer asked for two more beers.

"Is Lily working tonight?" he asked as the bartender brought the fresh beers.

"Who wantsta know?" the barkeep asked.

"I do," Palmer said. "A friend of mine said she's the top girl here. That's what I want."

"What friend?"

"The kind who doesn't want to have his name tossed around," Palmer said. "He's got a scar here." Palmer ran his finger down his face.

The bartender's eyes widened.

"You know who I mean?" Palmer asked.

"Lily is the redhead," the bartender said, looking across the room. "She deals blackjack."

"She's not a saloon girl?"

"No."

"Okay," Palmer said, "but do you know—"

"I've got work to do."

The bartender moved away.

"He knows Dancy, and he's afraid of him," Palmer said to Atlee.

"Do you wanna make him talk more?"

"No," Palmer said. "At least we know this is where Dancy comes, and the redhead is his woman. She's the one we need to talk to."

"Okay," Atlee said. "I'll follow your lead. When do we talk to her?"

"There's no time like the present."

A S PALMER WALKED over to the blackjack table, Atlee hung back and watched, just in case Dancy was in the crowd somewhere. So far the younger man had done everything he said he'd do, so Palmer was going to have to rely on him to watch his back.

As he got to the table, the single player who had been seated there got up and left, shaking his head.

"Guess he didn't have much luck, huh?" Palmer asked the pretty redhead.

"Luck had nothin' to do with it," she said. "He had no skill." She looked at him, and he was shocked by how green her eyes were. "How about you, cowboy? Skill or luck?"

"Neither," he said, sitting on a stool. "Information."

"I don't trade in information," she said, "but just for fun, what're you lookin' for?"

"Not what," Palmer said, "who?"

"Okay, then," she said, shuffling her cards, "who're you lookin for?"

"A man named Dancy."

She paused her shuffling, then continued.

"Never heard of him."

"Oh, yeah, you have," Palmer said. "He talks about you all the time."

"Is that right?" Her curiosity got the better of her. "What's he say?"

"How beautiful you are," Palmer answered. "Only he doesn't have the words to describe you. You're even more beautiful than I imagined."

"When did you see him last?" she asked.

"Oh, a few weeks ago," Palmer said. "We were supposed to meet up here. When did you see him last?"

"Oh, probably months," she said. "Did you know he expects me to be alone until he comes back?"

"A woman like you? Alone?" Palmer asked. "I can't imagine it."

She laughed.

"Neither can I."

"Maybe," Palmer said, "you and me, we can wait for him together."

"You would suggest that?" she asked. "Knowing I'm his woman?"

"Like you said," Palmer answered, "it's been months."

"You know," she said, putting the cards down and leaning her elbows on the table, "you're not bad-lookin'. We could go upstairs."

She was a blackjack dealer, not a saloon girl and not a whore. The only reason he could think for inviting him upstairs was if Dancy was already there.

"That sounds like an offer I can't refuse," he told her.

She smiled and lifted her hand over her head. A man immediately appeared; his sleeves were rolled up and he wore a visor.

"Take over," she said.

"Right, Lily."

"Follow me, handsome," she said, all of a sudden giving him a full sexy look with those eyes.

She started walking and he turned to follow. At the same time, he gave Atlee a signal he hoped the younger man would read properly.

Lily led him across the busy saloon floor to a stairway, and he followed her swaying hips up. When they reached the upstairs hallway, the noise from downstairs became muffled. Palmer drew his gun and grabbed Lily's arm as she stopped in front of a room.

"Is he inside?" he asked.

"What? Well, no— Hey, what's the gun for?"

"Stand aside," he told her as Atlee appeared at the

end of the hall. He kept his voice down as he told Atlee, "Keep an eye on the stairs."

"Right."

He looked at Lily, saw her take a deep breath.

"If you scream, he'll get shot and so will you," he told her.

She stopped in midbreath.

Gun in hand, Palmer lifted his foot and kicked out at the door. As it snapped open, he sprang into the room with his gun held out. The man lounging on the bed sat up quickly, eyes wide, then started for his gun, which was hanging on the bedpost.

"Don't do it!" Palmer shouted.

The man froze. Palmer could see the livid scar that ran down his face.

"Who the hell're you?" he growled.

"My name's Abe Cassidy."

"I don't know you."

Palmer took the badge from his pocket and held it out. "Maybe this'll help."

Jack Dancy squinted his eyes.

"You're the marshal from Integrity?"

"That's right."

"You got no official standing here," Dancy said.

"I'm taking you back with me, anyway, Dancy," Palmer said.

"My boys are downstairs," Dancy said. "You'll never get me to the door."

"I'm sure they're having a good time," Palmer said. "They won't notice us taking you out the back door."

Dancy frowned and Palmer could see him considering going for the gun.

He cocked the hammer on his gun.

"Roll off the bed to your right, Dancy," Palmer said since the gun was hanging on the left post.

Dancy hesitated, then rolled off the bed to his feet. Palmer walked to the bedpost and plucked the gun from the holster. He stuck it in his belt, then gestured with his gun.

"We're going to walk to the other end of the hall," he said, hoping he would find a customary back way out there.

"When they miss me," Dancy said, "my boys will come lookin'."

"Hopefully we'll be long gone by then."

"In the dark?" Dancy asked.

"We'll be real careful."

As they came out of the room, Lily said, "Jack, I'm sorry—"

Dancy backhanded her across the face, almost knocking her down. She slumped against the wall, her hand to her face.

"Stupid bitch, you brought him up here?"

"I thought—"

"You ain't supposed to think!"

Her face grew red.

"I hope they hang you!"

Palmer looked down the hall.

"Steve, let's go."

Atlee came trotting down the hall.

"Put her in the room," he told him.

"Should I tie her up?"

Lily still had her hand to her face, a murderous expression on her beautiful face.

"I don't think so," Palmer said. She looked angry

enough to let them take Dancy out the back. Later she might regret it, but one way or another, Dancy's boys would come after them. Tying her up might alleviate her anger toward Dancy and instead make her mad at Palmer and Atlee. "I don't think he should've hit that beautiful face."

"I don't think so, either," she said.

"Come on, ma'am," Atlee said, walking her into the room. "Now you just sit there a while."

"Don't worry," she said. "You can have 'im."

When they got to the far end of the hall, they found another staircase going down.

"You go ahead of us and bring the horses around back," Palmer said.

"What about his horse?" Atlee asked. "We don't know which one it is."

Lily stuck her head out of her room and said, "It's a roan."

"Shut up, bitch!" Dancy snapped.

She smiled and withdrew her head.

"Grab the roan," Palmer said to Atlee.

"Right."

Atlee ran down the steps ahead of them.

"Walk easy, Dancy," Palmer said. "I won't mind putting a bullet in your back. The lady you shot was a friend of mine."

"That bastard Henderson's wife?" Dancy said. "She just got in the way. Too bad, she wasn't bad-lookin'."

"Well, that lady's going to put you away, Dancy, when she testifies."

"She ain't dead?"

"No, she's not."

They reached the bottom and were in a hallway with a door at the far end.

"Keep walking," Palmer said. "First move you make to get away, you're dead."

"I got time," Dancy said. "It's a long way back to Integrity."

CHAPTER TWENTY

WHEN PALMER GOT out back with Dancy, Atlee was there, mounted on his horse and holding the reins of two others.

"Get on the roan," Palmer told Dancy.

Atlee drew his gun and covered Dancy while Palmer mounted his gelding. When they were all mounted, Palmer tied Dancy's hands in front of him. If he tied them behind the man, he might fall out of the saddle.

"If you try to ride off, you'll be dead before you get ten feet. Got it?"

"I got it," Dancy said. "I just have to wait for my boys to set me free."

"If they come after us, I'll take them in, too," Palmer said.

Dancy laughed and said, "We'll see."

"Yeah, we will," Palmer said. "Steve, you take the lead. Let's get out of town."

"Right."

T HEY RODE HARD out of town, but when they had left the lights behind, they slowed.

"I can't ride in the dark hog-tied like this," Dancy complained.

"Do the best you can," Palmer said. "At least I didn't tie your hands behind your back." He looked at Atlee. "We need a place to camp."

"I can ride up ahead," Atlee said.

"Good. Find something out of sight, or we'll have to make a cold camp. And it's cold enough."

"Right."

As Atlee rode on ahead, Dancy started talking.

"Why would you come all this way to take me back?" he asked. "Your badge is no good here."

"Maybe not," Palmer said, "but my gun will still do the trick."

"Against all my boys?" Dancy said. "There are four of them, you know."

"Three," Palmer said. "Pike's already on his way back."

"Oh, you caught Pike, huh?" Dancy said.

"And he wasn't very happy about being left behind," Palmer said. "He's going to do a lot of talking."

"That's okay," Dancy said. "He don't know nothin'."

"Oh, we'll take what little he does know," Palmer said, "and put it together with what Belle Henderson tells us. That'll be enough to build a case against you and get you hanged."

"You ain't gonna hang me, Marshal," Dancy said.

Palmer took his badge from his pocket and pinned it on.

"We'll see," he said.

They heard a horse approaching them from ahead, and Palmer reined in. There was enough moonlight for him to see Atlee.

"I found a spot," he said.

"Lead on."

They followed Atlee to a clearing that was surrounded by rocks.

"We can make a fire here that won't be seen from far off," Atlee said.

"Good," Palmer said. "I'll build the fire. You take care of the horses."

"And him?"

"We'll tie his hands behind him," Palmer said.

"How am I supposed to eat that way?" Dancy asked.

"Who says you're gonna eat?" Palmer asked.

He got the fire going, put on a pot of coffee for them to have with their beef jerky. They had restocked at a small-town mercantile along the way, but just coffee and jerky. Nothing to slow them down.

Atlee picketed the horses and came to the fire. Palmer handed him a cup of coffee and a hunk of jerky.

"Hey!" Dancy called. "I'm hungry, and I'm cold."

They had set him down away from the fire and the warmth of it, but within the glow of it so they could watch him.

"That cold you feel is comin' from inside you," Atlee said. "From your heart."

"Yeah, yeah . . ." Dancy said. "At least let me have some coffee."

"Just shut up," Palmer said. "You killed an innocent man and shot his wife. You don't deserve any consideration."

Dancy started to laugh.

"Innocent?" he asked. "You think Eddie Dickson was innocent?"

"Dickson?" Palmer asked. "You killed Ken Henderson."

"Henderson, that's the name he took to live in Integrity," Dancy said. "But when we were partners, he was Eddie Dickson."

"He was your partner?"

"For ten years," Dancy said. "Until we pulled a job that was big enough for him to turn on me. It took me years to find him in Integrity, where he used the money to open a business and get married. But he was a liar and a phony. Had the people of Integrity totally fooled."

Palmer stared at Dancy, for a moment thinking the killer could have been talking about him.

"He was worse than I was when we were partners," Dancy went on. "If anythin', he made me what I am today."

"Whatever was between the two of you," Palmer said, "you killed a citizen of Integrity, and I'm taking you back."

"That coffee smells good," Dancy said. "One cup and I'll shut up."

Atlee looked at Palmer, who nodded. They tied Dancy's hands in front again and gave him a cup of coffee. He sipped from it gratefully.

"You think he's tellin' the truth?" Atlee asked as they sat by the fire. "About Henderson?"

"I don't know," Palmer said. "Maybe Belle does. We can ask her when we get back."

"If she's alive," Atlee said.

"She'll be alive," Palmer said.

They finished their coffee and a meal of jerky, took the cup away from Dancy, and tied his hands behind him again.

"You're gonna make me sleep like this?" the killer asked. "I can't."

"Give it a try," Palmer told him. "Steve, I'll take the first watch."

"Fine with me," Atlee said. "I can use some shut-eye."

Atlee rolled himself up in his blanket and bedroll. Palmer hunkered down by the fire, holding his rifle across his knees and a cup of coffee in his hand.

He thought about what Dancy had said about Ken Henderson being a liar and a phony. The words hit home. But maybe if he managed to get Dancy back to Integrity to pay for what he'd done, he'd be less of a phony.

He wondered if Dancy was right about his men. Would the three remaining try to catch up to them and free him? Or would they be glad he was gone? Dancy probably didn't treat his men any better than he treated his woman.

Palmer poured himself another cup of coffee and kept a sharp eye on their back trail.

PALMER CAME AWAKE abruptly as Steve Atlee shook him.

"Time to get up, Marshal."

Palmer came out of his bedroll quickly, got to his feet, and looked around. He was relieved when he saw Dancy still there and still hog-tied.

"Here," Atlee said, and handed Palmer a cup of coffee.

"That's it," Palmer said. "Just coffee and then let's move."

"Coffee for Dancy?" Atlee asked.

"No," Palmer said. "Let's just get him ready to move."

While Atlee did that, Palmer climbed up on some rocks so he could get a good look behind them. As far as the eye could see, there was no sign of Dancy's men. Palmer dropped down to the ground and told Atlee they were clear.

"Sure," Dancy said with a grin, "for now."

Between them they got Dancy on his horse and then mounted up themselves.

"You want me to scout ahead today," Atlee asked, "or keep an eye on our back trail?"

"Back trail," Palmer said. "If they come at us, it's going to be from behind, not from ahead."

"Right."

"It's at least three days from here to Integrity," Dancy told them. "In that much time, anything can happen."

"You'd just better be wrong," Palmer said, "because if something does happen, the first thing I'm going to do is put a bullet in your brain."

Dancy laughed.

"You ain't gonna get me hung that way!" he snapped.

"Maybe not," Palmer said, "but I'll be just as happy to leave you dead by the side of the road."

CHAPTER TWENTY-ONE

T WO DAYS OF traveling were uneventful.
   On the third day Atlee came riding in from checking their back trail.

"They're comin'," he said.

"I told you," Dancy said, smiling. "They're good boys."

Palmer ignored the man.

"How many?"

"Three, like he said."

Actually, Dancy had said four, but Palmer had reminded him that Pike had already been caught.

"How far behind us are they?"

"About an hour."

"They must have been making good time."

Palmer had stopped to rest the horses. Now Palmer said to Atlee, "All right, you go on ahead with him. I'll take care of them."

"All three?" Atlee asked. "Why don't we tie him to a tree or somethin', and we'll both handle 'em."

"Just do it my way, Steve," Palmer said.

"Okay, yeah, you're the boss."

He grabbed the reins of Dancy's horse and started off with the outlaw in tow.

Palmer mounted up and started riding back.

W HEN PALMER SPOTTED the three riders in the distance, he reined in, dismounted, and found some high ground. His original plan was to bushwhack the three men, kill them, and then head back to Integrity. But now he realized there was no way he could be sure these were Dancy's men. What if they were just three riders riding this way coincidentally? He couldn't kill them without finding out for sure they were killers.

He hid his horse, tied it to a tree, and climbed up atop an outcropping of rocks that would give him the drop on them.

And he waited.

T HE THREE MEN were riding at a brisk pace, which was probably why they had gotten this close. Palmer sighted down the barrel of his rifle, waiting until they got closer, feeling sure these were Dancy's men, but not sure enough to pull the trigger. Finally, they were below him and he shouted, "That's far enough!"

They reined in and began looking around with their hands on their guns.

"Just stand easy," Palmer said. "Don't go for your guns. You're covered."

The three men looked up toward his voice.

"You're Dancy's men," Palmer said.

The three men stared at him, then at one another. Finally one of them said, "Where is he?"

"Oh, he's on his way back to Integrity to hang."

"We can't let ya take 'im," another said.

"Well, actually, I mean to take all of you back," Palmer told them. "You're all involved in the murder of Ken Henderson."

"Naw, naw," the third said, "that was all Dancy. He told us we was robbin' the place. Then we go in and he shoots that fella and his wife."

"And you didn't know anything about it?" Palmer said.

"That's right," the man said.

"So tell me," Palmer said, "why are you tracking us? Why do you want Dancy?"

"He's the boss," one said.

Another shrugged and said, "What else should we do?"

"Forget him," Palmer said. "Go your separate ways. Start over."

They exchanged glances.

"You'd let us do that?"

"I'm just saying that's what you should've done. Now that we're all here, I've got to take you in."

"We can't let ya do that," one repeated.

"You don't have a choice."

They all smiled.

"All we got to do is skin our hoglegs and start shooting. It's three against one."

"But I've already got you covered," Palmer pointed out. "I'll kill two of you before you get your guns out.

Then me and the third one'll dance, and we'll see what happens."

"You seem pretty sure."

"I've been in situations like this before," Palmer told them. "I know how they turn out."

The three men looked at one another again.

"Now all you've got to do is drop your pistols and rifles to the ground, and come quietly."

"You think you can get us all back to Integrity?" one asked.

"I think I sure can try."

The three exchanged still another look, and then Palmer saw one nod.

"Don't—," he started, but they all went for their guns.

Palmer fired his rifle twice. One man flew from his saddle as if he'd been roped from behind. The second man took a bullet in the shoulder. The third man leaped off his horse and rolled toward cover.

Palmer ducked back out of sight. He'd killed one, and there were two left, one wounded, one not. Not quite the way he'd figured it.

"Marshal!" somebody yelled. "You didn't get two of us, so you're still outnumbered."

Palmer didn't answer.

"So now the dance is two to one," the voice shouted, and then laughed.

Palmer thought he could stay where he was. If they tried to climb up after him, he'd pick them off. Of course, if they decided to wait him out, they had water and his canteen was on his saddle. So he had to make a move.

First, he had to get off that rock down to even footing with them. One of them was bleeding, probably pretty bad, so the two to one was more like one and a half to one.

Palmer slid down the back of the rock, the way he had come up. His horse was about a hundred yards away, but that was not where he wanted to go. He could have ridden off and left the men on foot, but they'd always be looking over their shoulder. He had to finish it here.

The best way to finish this was head-on. He had to step out into the open and have them reveal their position. After that, it was going to come down to whoever could shoot the quickest and most accurately. Palmer had never been a fast gun, but he usually hit what he shot at.

He listened, thought he could hear some movement, then stepped out from behind the rock base, gun ready. There was nothing. He took a few steps slowly, then more quickly, then stopped and listened. Still nothing. Then he heard a horse and ducked back, but when the animal went by, there was no one in the saddle. The two men might've lost both their horses. He was going to have to take care of them before they found his gelding.

Holding his rifle ready, he continued forward, stopped when he saw the blood on the ground.

"Come on out," he called. "Let's finish this." He waited, got no answer. "You must want to do this or you wouldn't have gone for your guns. Come on, here I am."

Then he saw the other horses, two of them, off in the distance. Maybe he could've stayed where he was. Their water was on their saddle, and their horses were loose.

"Okay," somebody called, "let's do it! We'll step out."

He turned, tried to see where the voices were coming from.

"Come on, then," he said.

He looked around, then saw the first man step out. Behind him came the second, bleeding from one shoulder.

"We can call this off," Palmer said. "Drop your guns and come with me."

"We ain't gonna dangle from no rope," the uninjured man said.

Palmer looked at the bleeding man. Probably a few more moments and he'd collapse. He looked pale, and his injured arm was dangling.

The uninjured man went for his gun and Palmer shot him in the chest. Then he levered another round and pointed the rifle at the bleeding man.

"You'll have to take your hand away from your wound to draw your gun," Palmer said. "Either way, you're going to die."

The other man stared at him, opened his mouth to speak, and then suddenly slumped to the ground. Palmer went to him and leaned over him. He was dead. His wound had bled profusely, and he couldn't survive. Palmer checked both of the other men, found them both dead. He left them where they were, not wanting to take the time to bury them. He walked to his horse, mounted up, and rode away.

W HAT'S YOUR STORY?" Dancy asked Atlee as they rode along.

"Whataya mean?"

"I mean," Dancy said, "why're you doin' this? You're no lawman."

"I'm a deputy," Atlee insisted.

"Without a badge?"

"I'll get one when we get back," Atlee said. "There was no time. We had to ride after you."

"A posse?"

"Just three of us," Atlee said.

"Look," Dancy said, "why be a deputy? I've got plenty of money hidden away. It's yours. All we have to do is go and get it."

"I wanna be a deputy," Atlee said. "I don't want your money."

"You're crazy, then," Dancy said. "That's the only explanation. The marshal, it's his job, but you . . . you're just crazy."

"Shut up," Atlee said.

"Why?" Dancy said. "You gonna kill me? The marshal wants to take me back alive."

"I'll tell 'im you tried to escape," Atlee said. "You tried for my gun, and I had to shoot you. Then we'll just take your body back to town. So shut up."

"I'm shuttin' up," Dancy said, "but believe me, son, your time's gonna come."

LATER, ATLEE HEARD the horse behind them, reined in, and turned.

"My boys," Dancy said with a smile.

"One horse," Atlee said. "It's the marshal."

They both looked and waited, finally saw Palmer riding toward them. Atlee looked over at Dancy, saw the blank look on his face.

"What happened?" Atlee asked.

"I found them," Palmer told him, "and I took care of them."

"You killed all of them?" Dancy demanded.

Palmer turned to face the man.

"They didn't give me a choice."

"I'm gonna make you pay for that, lawman," Dancy growled at him.

"I'd like to see you try," Palmer said, "from the end of a rope." He looked at Atlee. "Let's get this polecat back to Integrity."

CHAPTER TWENTY-TWO

PALMER TURNED THE key in the lock and stared through the cell bars at Jack Dancy.

"Welcome home," he said.

"You ain't gonna leave me here with him, are ya?" Pike shouted.

"There's an empty cell between you," Palmer said. "I think you'll be fine."

When he came out of the cellblock, Steve Atlee was seated at his desk, and Mayor O'Connor was standing in front of the desk, eyeing Atlee suspiciously.

"Mr. Mayor," Palmer said.

"Marshal," O'Connor said, "that's the man who shot Henderson?"

"He was the leader of the men who came to town when Henderson was shot," Palmer said. "He said he shot him, and we'll know more when we can talk to Belle Henderson."

O'Connor looked at Atlee again.

"Steve," Palmer said, "open up that drawer on the right. There are a couple of deputy's badges in there. Pin one on."

"Yessir!"

"Marshal—" O'Connor started.

"I wouldn't have that man in a cell," Palmer said, "and the men who were with him wouldn't be dead without Deputy Atlee, Mr. Mayor. I think he deserves a badge, don't you?"

O'Connor looked at Atlee, who was pinning on the badge, and then back at Palmer.

"It's your call, Marshal. Please let me know what you find out from Mrs. Henderson."

The mayor turned and left.

"Marshal, why didn't you tell him Henderson's real name?" Atlee asked.

"The man had a new life here," Palmer said. "Besides, we've got only the word of a killer that he had another name."

"What happens if Belle Henderson says Dancy didn't shoot her husband?" Atlee asked.

"Then I guess we're in trouble," Palmer said. "But I'm going to go find out right now. You stay here and watch the prisoners, Deputy."

"Yessir!"

PALMER FOUND OUT from Doc Stack that Belle Henderson was alive and resting at home. The Hendersons had a small house in a section of town that looked like it was in need of a cleanup. His knock on the door was answered by a woman he recognized as Reba Waters, the sometime nurse for Doc Stack.

"Marshal," she greeted him.

"How is she?"

"Weak and resting but alive," Reba said. "I'm tryin' to get her to eat somethin'. I'm glad you're back. Did you get the man?"

"I believe we did," Palmer said, "but I need to talk to her to find out for sure."

"Well, she'll be glad to see you," Mrs. Waters said.

The inside of the house was neat, looked to be furnished with handmade chairs and tables. There was a second, small room that served as the bedroom. Palmer crossed to the doorway and looked in. Belle Henderson was lying on her back with a sheet covering her. Mrs. Waters must have spent time combing her hair for her, for she looked lovely, although pale.

He entered the room and approached the bed.

"Belle?"

She didn't respond immediately.

"Belle," he said again, and this time her eyes fluttered and then opened.

"Marshal?"

"That's right."

"Is it really you?"

"In the flesh."

"I'm sorry," she said. "I've been havin' dreams, and I'm never sure what's real and what isn't." She put her hand out and he took it.

"I'm real," he assured her. "Can you answer some questions?"

"I think so."

"I really only have one," Palmer said. "Do you know who shot you and your husband?"

"Y-yes," she said. "The man I saw with Ken, the one with the . . . the scar down his face."

"That's all I needed to know," Palmer said, squeezing her hand.

"D-did you get him?" she asked.

"I got him," he said. "He's in a cell, and he's going to hang."

Now she squeezed his hand.

"Thank you."

He patted her hand and then released it.

"You rest," he said. "When you're well enough, you'll testify and put him away."

"Yes," she said, and closed her eyes.

He didn't bother asking her if she knew her husband had had another name. Maybe Henderson had fooled her along with everyone else.

The way he was doing.

IT WAS A week later when Belle Henderson walked hesitantly into a courtroom and testified against Jack Dancy for shooting her and her husband.

"Your Honor," Dancy's attorney said, "this woman is obviously not recovered enough from her injuries to make a proper identification."

"Counselor," the judge said, "sit down!"

It seemed like moments later that the jury came in with a guilty verdict.

"Mr. Dancy, please stand," the judge said. "You have been found guilty of murder in the first degree.

I'm not going to put this off because I don't want to come back here to do it. You are hereby sentenced to be hanged by the neck until you are dead. The hanging will take place just as soon as a scaffold can be erected and a hangman brought to town." He banged his gavel. "This court is adjourned."

O UTSIDE THE COURTROOM Belle was waiting for Palmer; she grabbed both his hands the moment she saw him. Deputy Atlee stood off to one side with both prisoners, Dancy and Pike. Both men had their hands shackled behind them, but Pike still looked nervous.

"Thank you so much," she said.

"I told you," Palmer replied. "He's going to hang for what he did."

Palmer left her and went to help Steve Atlee take Dancy and Pike back to their cells.

"You must be pretty pleased with yourself," Dancy said as Palmer locked the cell door.

"You got that right, Dancy," Palmer said. "You're getting what you deserve."

"Did you tell the pretty wife what her husband's real name was?"

"No," Palmer said, "and you won't, either."

"Don't you think the people here deserve to know what a phony they had living among them?"

"I don't," Palmer said. "I believe a man deserves a new start."

"Now," Dancy said, "why would you believe somethin' like that?"

Palmer ignored him and left the cellblock.

"He still don't think he's gonna hang, huh?" Atlee asked.

"He's in for a big disappointment," Palmer said.

"You wanna take some time off, Marshal?" Atlee asked. "I can handle things from here."

"No, that's okay," Palmer said. "I'm not taking any time off until he's swinging."

"Well, then," Atlee said, grabbing his hat, "I think I'll go for a drink and somethin' to eat."

"Don't spend a lot of time in a saloon," Palmer told him. "One drink and out. Got it?"

"Got it."

Atlee left and Palmer sat at his desk. He was wanted in most of the Southwest. He considered what he was doing in Integrity, South Dakota, starting over. But he would hate to think of himself as a phony. He was lying, yes, but he was doing it to have a life. By becoming Marshal Abe Cassidy, he didn't feel he was taking anything away from anyone. After all, the real Cassidy and his family were all dead.

But one thought nagged at him. It had appeared when he found the Cassidy family and their wagons that there might have been more children than the ones who had been killed. What if one or two children had been taken by the Indians? Were they out there believing their father would be coming for them? Was he doing them a disservice by not searching for them? He didn't think so. After all, he wasn't their real father.

He thought about going to the stove for some coffee, but instead took a bottle of whiskey from his bottom drawer.

* * *

"H EY, MARSHAL!" DANCY shouted from his cell.
     "Shut up!" Palmer shouted back.

"Come on," Dancy said, "I'm hungry. Don't I get fed?"

"What's it matter?" Palmer asked. "You're going to hang."

"Not on an empty stomach, I ain't!"

Palmer looked at the bottle of whiskey on his desk. He had already consumed too much of it, so he put it back in his desk drawer. Something to eat would probably be a good idea for him, too. At that moment, Steve Atlee came walking in.

"You ready for supper, Marshal?" he asked.

"I was just thinking about that, Deputy," Palmer said, standing. "When I come back, I'll bring the prisoners something, so if Dancy starts yelling again about being hungry, tell him to be patient."

"Got it."

Palmer put on his hat and left the office, heading for the Stallion or the Sweetwater.

CHAPTER TWENTY-THREE

A STEAK AT THE Sweetwater helped soak up the whiskey Palmer had drank in his office. He was still wondering if Belle Henderson deserved to know about her husband's former life. And could he wonder about something like that while he was keeping his true identity from an entire town?

After he finished eating, he asked the waiter to put two meals together for the prisoners. The man did so and brought them out in a basket.

"You can bring the knives and forks back whenever you come in again, Marshal," the man said.

"I'd appreciate if you cut the steak up now," Palmer said. "I'm not giving my prisoners knives."

"Sure thing, Marshal."

He carried the basket back to the jail and into the cellblock.

"That my supper?" Dancy asked. "Finally?"

"I got you a steak," Palmer said. "Stand against the back wall."

Dancy backed up until he was flat against the wall. Palmer unlocked the door, set the basket down on the floor, put a cup of water next to it, and then locked the door. He walked over and did the same with Pike.

Dancy picked up the basket and took it to his cot. The first thing he did was take out the fork.

"How am I supposed to eat a steak without a knife?" he asked.

"The steak's already been cut up for you."

Dancy took the plate out and saw what Palmer meant.

"I gotta admit, Marshal, you think of everythin'," Dancy said.

"Shut up and eat," Palmer said. "Let me know when you're done."

"Sure thing, Marshal."

Palmer left the cellblock, went to the stove, and poured himself a cup of coffee.

"You can go home, Steve," he said, walking to the desk. "I'll see you in the morning."

"You gonna spend the night here, Marshal?"

Palmer nodded.

"I can sleep at my desk."

"I'll relieve you early so you can get some breakfast and then some proper sleep," Atlee said.

"That sounds good, Deputy," Palmer said. "Good night."

"'Night, Marshal."

Atlee left and Palmer leaned back in his chair. He was more than two months into his new life as Marshal Abe Cassidy. If he decided to move, would he have to take on another name or go back to being Tom Palmer?

He knew he didn't want to go back to an outlaw life. Twenty years was enough. With his last job going bad, he had come full circle from when he was sixteen. If he left now and he wasn't an outlaw or a lawman, what would he be? His only experiences were on either side of the law.

"Marshal!" Dancy shouted.

"What?"

"I'm finished," Dancy said, "but I can smell that coffee. I sure could use a cup."

Palmer gave it some thought, then went to the stove and poured a cup. He carried it into the cellblock. Dancy had placed the basket on the floor in front of the door.

"Back up," Palmer said.

Once again, Dancy pressed his back to the wall. Palmer opened the door, grabbed the basket, put the coffee cup down, and then closed the gate. Dancy came forward and picked up the cup. He held it so he could smell it.

"Thanks, Marshal."

He took it back to the cot, sat, and sipped slowly.

Palmer made a point of also giving Pike a cup.

"Thanks, Marshal," Pike said.

Palmer took the basket and left the cellblock, saying over his shoulder, "Don't call me anymore. Go to sleep." He closed the cellblock door and went back to his desk.

H E WOKE THE next morning with his head down on his desk and his back aching. He wondered what had awakened him when he heard Dancy shouting from the cellblock.

". . . breakfast sometime today? Marshal?"

"Damn it!" Palmer cursed to himself. "I should just ignore him."

Instead, he went to the cellblock door and opened it. "Stop shouting."

"I'm hungry," Dancy complained. "I need breakfast."

"You'll get breakfast when I get breakfast," Palmer said. "Both of you."

"I can wait, Marshal," Pike said.

"And when will that be?" Dancy asked.

"When my deputy shows up."

"And when's that supposed to happen?"

"Any minute now," Palmer said. "Until then . . . shut up!"

He started back to his desk, but at that moment, the office door opened and Deputy Steve Atlee entered.

"Sorry I'm late," the deputy said.

"You're not," Palmer told him. "You're right on time." He grabbed his hat. "I'll be back with breakfast for the prisoners after I have mine."

"I'm sure they'll be patient," Atlee said, "and wait."

Palmer left.

AFTER BREAKFAST PALMER went to his hotel room and slept for two hours, then got up, dressed, strapped on his gun, and stood in front of the mirror with the badge in his hand. He hesitated, put the badge in his shirt pocket, took it out, hesitated, then pinned it on.

He put on his hat then and left the room. He stopped at a small café and got some food wrapped in brown paper. When he walked back into the office, Atlee looked at him from his desk.

"He's been shoutin' all mornin'," Atlee said.

"Give them this." Palmer tossed the package to Atlee. "They're sandwiches."

Atlee carried it into the cellblock, passed it between the bars.

"This is it?" Dancy asked.

"You'd better be happy with that," Atlee said.

"Supper'd better be better," the prisoner said.

Atlee left the cellblock.

"You don't look rested, Marshal," he said.

"I got a couple of hours," Palmer said. "Why don't you go and make some rounds?"

"Yessir."

As Atlee left, Palmer sat at his desk. He stared and thought. He realized he had enjoyed hunting down Jack Dancy. He realized he liked being a town marshal. He didn't like being a liar, but he thought the longer he was Marshal Cassidy, the less that would bother him.

Palmer didn't like having Jack Dancy in his jail. He was reminded of Ken Henderson, who had another name. And Palmer had decided that was something Belle never needed to know. So the sooner they hanged Dancy, the better. Or he could let the man escape and then shoot him while he did so. But he doubted that was something a dedicated lawman would ever do.

He wanted to go and see the mayor, but couldn't do that until Atlee returned. Leaving a convicted murderer alone was definitely not something a dedicated lawman would do.

A TLEE RETURNED TWO hours later.
  "I'm going to see the mayor," Palmer said.

"Okay. What about supper for the prisoners?"

"I'll bring it back with me. Tell Dancy if he starts shouting, he doesn't get fed."

"I will."

Palmer went to city hall. The mayor saw him immediately.

"How's the prisoner?" the mayor asked.

"Noisy, demanding, annoying," Palmer said.

"What brings you here?"

"When will he be hanged?"

"I've got carpenters starting on a gallows tomorrow," Mayor O'Connor said. "A hangman will be here in three days."

"So I've got to put up with him for three more days."

"Unless you want to let him escape and then shoot him in the act."

"I thought about that," Palmer said.

"And?"

"It's not something I'm comfortable with."

"So then I guess you're stuck with him for three more days."

"I'll just keep my eye on the prize," Palmer said. "You'll let me know if there's any change?"

"I'll keep you informed."

"Thanks, Mr. Mayor."

Palmer left the mayor's office and went to see Belle Henderson.

*   *   *

W HEN PALMER KNOCKED on Belle's door, he was surprised that she opened it herself.

"Where's Mrs. Waters?"

"I sent her back to work," she said. "Coffee?"

"I can get it if you want to sit."

"No," she said, "I'll get it. Sit at the table."

He sat and watched as she moved about the kitchen, slowly but deftly. He didn't think she was in much pain, just dealing with the shadow of it. He'd been shot a time or two. It took a while to realize you could move freely.

She carried two cups to the table and sat across from him. Her hair was pinned behind her head in a bun, and she was still pale, but also still lovely.

"What brings you here?" she asked.

"Dancy is going to hang in three days," he said. "I wanted to tell you that."

"I don't have to attend, do I?" she asked.

"No, not if you don't want to."

"I don't. I'll be satisfied to know that it was done."

"What's going to happen with the store?"

"Our employees are keeping it open while I recover," she said, "and then I'll go back. It's all I have."

"I thought— I mean, I was afraid . . ."

"What?"

"That you might want to leave town."

"No," she said, "this is my home. The town did nothing to me to make me feel otherwise. In fact, I've had visits from several neighbors who are offering to help."

"That's good," he said.

"I suppose it is," she said, "but they weren't very friendly or helpful while Ken was alive."

"Maybe they just didn't like him."

That seemed to surprise her.

"You might be right about that."

"Did he have many friends?" Palmer asked.

"No. In fact, he didn't have any. That's why I was surprised when I saw him with that man with the scar and asked him about it. He said he was just an old friend."

"I guess you'll never know for sure if they were friends."

"The man killed him," she said. "You don't kill your friends, do you?"

"Well . . . I don't."

He finished his coffee.

"I've got to get back to work," he said.

"And so do I," she said, standing. "Probably tomorrow."

"Are you sure you're ready?" he asked.

"I guess I'll find out," she said, and walked him to the door.

CHAPTER TWENTY-FOUR

THE DAY OF the hanging brought people to town from the surrounding area. Palmer had never been able to understand how such a morbid event could become a festive occasion. He had always stayed away from hangings, but that wasn't possible with this one, since he was bringing the guest of honor.

The mayor came into Palmer's office early that morning and said, "The hangman's here, so we're all set."

"Good. Is it always like this?"

"Like what?"

"A party."

"Don't they have necktie parties back East?" the mayor asked.

"Not like this," Palmer said. "Just walking from my hotel to here, I saw five times as many people as I usually do."

"Yes," the mayor said, "unfortunately, a hanging always brings them out. The hangman will be in to take measurements."

"That's fine."

The mayor left. It seemed like moments later a dour-looking man entered and said, "I'm Amos Hardwicke, the hangman."

"Ah," Palmer said, "you're here for your measurements."

"Yes," the man said, "I've already tested the gallows mechanism. I just need to finish up here."

Palmer stood up and said, "Then let's do it."

He led the way into the cellblock and called out, "You've got a visitor, Dancy."

The outlaw looked up from the cot, saw the man with Palmer, and understood.

THE NEXT TIME Palmer went into the block, he said, "It's time, Dancy."

The outlaw stood up.

"Turn around," Palmer said, and unlocked the door. He entered and applied chains to the killer's wrists.

"You know," Dancy said, "I never thought we'd get here."

"What did you expect?" Palmer asked.

Dancy turned around.

"I don't know," Dancy said. "Maybe I saw somethin' in you. . . . I thought you'd let me go."

"Why would you think that?"

"Because you're not like any lawman I ever knew," Dancy said.

"Well, I'm new to the job," Palmer said.

"So then you've never done . . . this?" Dancy asked.

"No," Palmer said, "this is my first hanging."

"That makes two of us."

PALMER WAS TROUBLED as he walked Dancy to the gallows. If the killer could see through him, what if other people could, too? Or was it just that he and Dancy had spent so much time on the same side of the law?

People crowded around the scaffold, but as Palmer and Dancy approached, they spread out and created a path for them. When the two men reached the stairs, the hangman was there waiting. There was also another man with a cleric's collar, holding a Bible. His name was Father Bennett, and he had tried to see Dancy earlier in the week, but the outlaw had turned him away.

"What are you doin' here?" Dancy asked him.

"I wanted to give you one last chance to make your peace—" the priest began, but Dancy turned away.

"Get him out of here," he said to Palmer. "I've already made my peace."

"Father," Palmer said, "he doesn't need you."

The priest, a man in his fifties who had devoted more than half his life to God, seemed puzzled.

"And you, Marshal?"

"To tell you the truth," Palmer said, "I don't need you, either."

The priest stared at both men, then turned and walked off.

The hangman, Hardwicke, went up the steps first, followed by Dancy, and then Palmer. At the top Palmer momentarily felt as if everyone was looking at him, but then he realized it was Dancy they were looking at. He moved Dancy onto the trapdoor, just beneath the noose, and then backed off. The hangman stepped forward and stood in front of Dancy.

"Do you have any last words?" he asked.

Dancy seemed to think a moment, then shrugged, and said, "I guess not."

"Do you want the hood?" Hardwicke asked.

"Why not?"

The hangman put a black hood over Dancy's head and then fitted the noose around his neck. He then stepped back, put his hand on the lever that controlled the trapdoor, and sprang it.

L ATER, PALMER WAS sitting in his office, replaying the hanging in his mind. Some of the people had actually applauded as Dancy's body fell through the trapdoor and the rope snapped his neck. Palmer thought there were those who were disappointed that Dancy hadn't danced at the end of the rope. Instead, he died instantly and simply dangled there.

The crowd finally began to break up when the undertaker cut the body down. There was nothing else to see. But as Palmer walked away, the few who were left patted him on the back as he went by.

He was not happy with the morning's events.

The door opened and Deputy Atlee came in.

"That was somethin'," he said.

"I'm sorry I didn't let you walk to the gallows with us," Palmer said.

"Don't be," Atlee said. "You looked miserable, and you still do. I don't think I missed anythin' from back in the crowd."

"You didn't, believe me," Palmer said.

"Was that your first?"

"Yes," Palmer said, "and I hope it was my last."

"Well, I have to tell you, it was a first for this town," Atlee said, "so maybe it *will* be your last."

"I guess I can hope so," Palmer said.

"You just did your job, you know," Atlee said.

"I know," Palmer said, "and now I'm going to do it some more. I'll make my rounds."

"I'll watch the office."

"We don't have any prisoners," Palmer pointed out.

"We still have Pike," Atlee said.

"Not for long," Palmer said. "He testified against Dancy, so the judge said I can let him go."

"And when are you gonna do that?"

"Now."

Palmer took the keys back to the cellblock and unlocked Pike's cell.

"What's goin' on?" Pike asked.

"You can go," Palmer told him.

"Who says?"

"The judge. He was impressed that you testified against Dancy."

They walked out of the cellblock, and Palmer gave him back his gun.

"Thanks, Marshal," Pike said.

"Take my advice and leave town," Palmer said.

"As soon as I can saddle my horse."

Pike left the office.

"*Now* we have no prisoners," Palmer said to Atlee.

"That's okay," Atlee said. "I like sittin' around the office. It gives me time to shine my badge."

"And you do keep it very shiny," Palmer admitted with a smile.

"I don't think I ever thanked you for givin' it to me," Atlee said.

"Well, you stepped up when nobody else would. You earned it. But . . ."

"But what?"

"I just realized there's somebody else I never thanked," Palmer said. "I'll see you later."

P ALMER ENTERED THE Palomino Saloon and approached the bar.

"Beer, Marshal?" Wade asked.

"Sure."

"I heard the hangin' went well," Wade said, setting the beer on the bar.

"I suppose it did, but hey," Palmer said, "I never thanked you for volunteering and riding out with me and Steve Atlee after that gang."

"That's okay, Marshal," Wade said. "It gave me a chance to take some time out from behind this bar. You know, stretch my legs."

"Well," Palmer said, "I wanted to say thanks."

"Anytime," Wade said. "Well, not anytime, but you know what I mean."

"Yeah, I do. Thanks for the beer."

P ALMER MADE HIS rounds of the town, which appeared to be getting back to normal after the hanging. If anything, the execution seemed to cement

Palmer's place in town. People were greeting him openly with smiles and respect. He might not have liked the hanging and might not have wanted to ever be involved with another one, but the result of this first one was more than he could have hoped for.

By the time he was finished with his rounds, he was feeling better about being Marshal Abe Cassidy. The town was finally accepting him, he had a deputy, and truth be told, he had a woman he was interested in. It would take a while for Belle to get over her husband's death, but he was willing to wait.

CHAPTER TWENTY-FIVE

Four months later . . .

LIEUTENANT DAN HENDRICKS reined in his horse and waited for his scout to reach him.

"Are they there?" he asked.

"Yes, sir, they are," Bob Eagle said.

"How many?" Hendricks asked.

"It looks like a dozen young braves, as well as some older ones, some squaws, and captives."

"Captives?"

Bob Eagle nodded.

"Whites."

Lieutenant Hendricks was leading a company of the 7th Cavalry out of Fort Meade in pursuit of a party of Sioux Indians who had been attacking white settlers and travelers over the past six to eight months. Bob

Eagle was one of the Crow scouts, called "wolves" by the Army.

Lieutenant Hendricks turned in his saddle and looked behind him at his sergeant and company of twenty men.

"Do we have enough men to engage them, Bob?" he asked the scout.

"I believe so, Lieutenant."

"How many captives do they have?"

"It looks like five or six, all white, some boys, some girls."

"Probably stole them after killing their parents," Hendricks said. "Sergeant!"

Sergeant Lester Muldoon, a career soldier in his fifties, came riding up alongside his young lieutenant.

"Sir?"

"Pass the word," Hendricks said. "We will be engaging a band of Sioux."

"Sir?"

"Bob has found a party that's holding captives," Hendricks said. "We are going to save them."

"Beggin' the lieutenant's pardon, but shouldn't we go back to Fort Meade for some more men?"

"That won't be necessary," Hendricks said. "Bob says there are about a dozen of them, along with some women and old men. I think we have enough men to handle them."

Sergeant Muldoon remembered when Custer felt the same way about a band of Sioux.

"I know what you're thinkin', Sergeant," Hendricks said. "This is not the Little Bighorn."

"Aye, sir, but—"

"No buts, Sergeant," Hendricks said. "Get the men

ready. We'll approach the camp in two groups. I'll lead one, you the other."

"Aye, sir." The Irishman turned his horse and rode back to inform the men.

LIEUTENANT HENDRICKS LED his group of ten to the top of a hill on one side of the Sioux camp. Across the way, at the top of a hill on the other side, he saw Sergeant Muldoon and his men. Down below, the Sioux had spotted them and were scrambling.

"Corporal," he called out, "have the bugler sound the charge."

"Yessir."

The sound of the bugle call was loud and floated across to the next hill. The sergeant and his men started down.

"Charge!" Lieutenant Hendricks called, and led his men down his hill.

The Sioux were still scrambling around when both groups of soldiers reached their camp. Hendricks was the first one to fire, and then all the soldiers began shooting. The Sioux had rifles, but only half of the braves had gotten to them, and they were firing ineffectually. The soldiers had taken them by surprise, and in moments, half of the young braves were dead. Unfortunately, the soldiers were firing indiscriminately, so some of the older Indians were soon lying dead, along with some of the squaws and children. The battle was over in moments, and silence fell over the camp.

The soldiers, once they had finished firing their guns, looked around with wide eyes, as if they had only just realized what they had done.

Sergeant Muldoon rode up alongside Lieutenant Hendricks.

"Most of them are dead, sir, and we have prisoners."

"And what about their prisoners?"

"We found some white captives in one of the tepees."

"Take me to them."

"Aye, sir."

Muldoon led Hendricks to a tepee where two privates were standing outside.

"Bring them out, Private," Muldoon said.

"Yes, sir."

The two soldiers went inside and came out with the white captives. There were about eight of them, mostly young boys, but also a couple of girls. The boys were bare to the waist, wearing loincloths, and the girls wore buckskin dresses. They all seemed frightened.

"Don't be scared," Hendricks said to them. "You've been rescued. We'll have you with your families in no time, but first we'll take you to Fort Meade. We have a doctor there who will examine you all." He turned to Muldoon. "Find some horses for these people."

"We can round up the Indian ponies that were scattered, sir," Muldoon said. "What about our prisoners?"

"They can walk back to the fort," Hendricks said.

"The women and children, too?"

"Yes," Hendricks said. "I want the horses to go to the white captives."

"Sir, there are some older braves and squaws who might not be able to make the walk."

"That's too bad."

"They might die on the way, sir."

"That would also be too bad, wouldn't it, Sergeant?"

"I don't believe they understand English, sir."

"Have Bob Eagle explain the situation to them," Hendricks said. "And let me know when we're ready to leave. I want to make the fort by nightfall."

"That might not be possible, sir," Muldoon said.

"It definitely won't be possible if we don't get started, Sergeant."

"Aye, sir."

THEY HAD TO camp overnight to keep the women, children, and older men from falling by the wayside. It was Sergeant Muldoon who convinced the lieutenant to stop for the night. By midday the following day they entered Fort Meade.

The prisoners were taken to the stockade, the rescued captives to the doctor, and Lieutenant Hendricks reported to the commanding officer, Colonel Harold Stockton.

"How many rescued?" the colonel asked when Hendricks finished his report.

"Eight," Hendricks said, "six boys, two girls. They're all almost teenagers."

"The Sioux like to take them in young," Stockton said. "Let's see if they remember who their parents are."

"I'll talk to the doctor," Hendricks said.

"Ask him to make a list," Stockton said. "I'd like to get them back to their families."

"We'll have to see how long they've been with the Sioux," Hendricks said, "how indoctrinated they've become."

"Work with the doctor on this, Lieutenant," Stockton said, "and get back to me."

* * *

WHEN LIEUTENANT HENDRICKS entered the doctor's quarters, Captain Sam Torrence looked over at him. He stuck both hands into the pockets of his white coat.

"I'm workin' on them," he said. "So far they seem healthy enough."

"How are their memories?" Hendricks asked. "How long have they been with the Sioux?"

"There are a couple who were there since early childhood," Doctor Torrence said. "I don't think they remember their families."

"And the others?"

"I still have to ask them," Torrence said. "I'm not sure they trust us yet."

"Maybe I should talk to them."

"No offense, Lieutenant, but your bedside manner leaves a lot to be desired. Leave it to me."

"All right, but the CO wants the answers fast," Hendricks said. "He wants to get these kids back to their families."

"I'll try to get somethin' from them today."

"Keep me informed, will you, Captain?"

"I will, Lieutenant."

CHAPTER TWENTY-SIX

WHEN THE CAVALRY rode down the main street of Integrity, they attracted a lot of attention. It had been a long time since the Army came to town.

The soldiers stopped in front of city hall and dismounted.

"Sergeant," Lieutenant Hendricks said, "the men can have one drink, and that's it. Understood?"

"Understood, sir."

"And no fights. Is that understood?"

"Aye, sir."

"I'll hold you responsible."

"Yes, sir!"

Hendricks turned and went into city hall.

Sergeant Muldoon went over to Corporal Agarn and said, "One drink per man, Corporal. That's an order."

"Yes, sir."

"And no fights," Muldoon said. "I'm holdin' you responsible."

"Yessir!"

Inside city hall the mayor immediately saw Lieutenant Hendricks in his office.

"What brings the Army to Integrity, Lieutenant?" Mayor O'Connor asked.

"We recently rescued some white captives from a band of Sioux Indians," the lieutenant said. "We wiped out their camp and took the rescued captives to Fort Meade."

"Well, that's good news. But how does that affect us here?"

"Do you have a marshal named Abraham Cassidy?"

"Yes, we do," O'Connor said. "He's been the law here for about six months now."

"And where did he come from?"

"Back East. He was traveling here with his entire family when they were set upon by a band of Sioux." O'Connor suddenly became excited. "Oh, my God, they killed his wife and his children. Are you saying—"

"One of the boys we rescued was able to tell us his name was Cassidy. He said his father was on the way here to take the marshal's job when they were attacked by Sioux. He said they killed his entire family and took him away."

"My God," O'Connor said, "so he's the marshal's son? He'll be thrilled, but . . ."

"But what?"

"The marshal also said his entire family was killed and he buried them."

"Then I suppose we'd better put them together and see what happens, shouldn't we?" Hendricks suggested.

"I guess we should."

"Where is he?" the lieutenant asked.

"He's out of town right now," O'Connor said, "at the Bar W."

"The Bar W?"

"Franklin Waverly's spread," O'Connor said, "the biggest spread in the county. A couple of his men got out of hand last night. Rather than hold them in a cell, Marshal Cassidy decided to take them back to their boss."

"When will he be back?"

"Later today. Why don't you and your men enjoy the hospitality of the town until then?"

"I might just take you up on that, Mr. Mayor," Hendricks said.

PALMER RODE UP to the Waverly house with the two ranch hands.

"You really gotta tell the boss what we did, Marshal?" one asked.

"I think I do," Palmer said.

"But . . . we might get fired," the other man said.

"Would you rather go back to jail?"

The two young men exchanged a glance, then shook their heads.

"Then we should get this over with," Palmer said.

As they all dismounted, a man came out of the barn and started walking over to them.

"Marshal," Ben Rogan said, "why are you here?"

"I'm bringing two of your men back to you," Palmer said.

"Back?" Rogan asked, folding his arms. "Where were they?"

"Jail."

"What'd they do?" Rogan looked at the two men, saw the bruises on their faces. "Who'd they get into a fight with?"

"Each other," Palmer said. "In the saloon. They caused quite a bit of damage."

"And you arrested them?"

"I did," Palmer said, "but I'm willing to release them if your boss will pay the damages."

"How much?" Rogan asked.

"A lot."

Rogan looked at the two men, who looked away.

"He might just wanna fire 'em," he said.

"Come on, boss," one of them whined.

"It'll have to come out of your pay," Rogan said.

"Sure, boss," the other man said.

Now Rogan looked at Palmer.

"Marshal, can they go back to work?" he asked.

"Sure," Palmer said. "I was going to talk to Mr. Waverly. . . ."

"I can do that," Rogan said. "He usually depends on me to discipline the men."

"Then they're all yours, Mr. Rogan."

"Thanks." Rogan looked at his men. "Go!"

One of them turned to Palmer and said, "Thanks, Marshal."

They walked away slowly, their shoulders hunched.

"They're good hands," Rogan said, "just a little young."

"I understand that," Palmer said. "Make sure they know next time they'll do jail time."

"I'll tell 'em."

Palmer nodded, mounted up, and headed back to town.

H E REACHED TOWN and took his horse right to the livery stable. When he came out, he found Steve Atlee waiting there for him.

"I been watchin' for you, Marshal."

"Something wrong, Steve?" he asked.

"I think you'd know better than me," the deputy said. "The Army's here lookin' for you."

"For me? Why?"

"I don't know, but the lieutenant who led them into town went right to the mayor's office."

"Where are they from?"

"I heard Fort Meade."

Palmer knew he wasn't wanted in South Dakota, and he'd never had anything to do with Fort Meade.

"I guess I'd better go and see the mayor," Palmer said.

"Most of the soldiers are in the Palomino."

"Good," Palmer said. "I'll stay away from there until I know what's going on."

"I'll go to the office, in case they come lookin' for you there. I'll tell 'em you're not back yet."

"Thanks, Steve."

They split up and Palmer headed for city hall.

* * *

H E SAID WHAT?" Palmer asked.

"He thinks they've rescued your son," the mayor said.

Palmer got a cold feeling in the pit of his stomach.

"Didn't you say the Sioux killed your entire family?" O'Connor asked.

"Yes," Palmer said, "I did say that."

"Then how could they have your son?"

"I don't know," Palmer said. "It may be a case of mistaken identity."

"But if you buried them all—"

"Mr. Mayor," Palmer said, "I took a hit on my head that day. I might have been . . . delirious."

"Well," O'Connor said, "you can talk to Lieutenant Hendricks. They can put you and the boy together and see if you recognize each other."

"That makes sense."

It made perfect sense, but he didn't know if he was going to be able to deny the truth if the boy said that Palmer wasn't his father, Abraham Cassidy.

"They said the boy was about eleven or twelve. Does that sound right?"

"Pretty close. Is he all right?"

"The lieutenant said he was confused at first and frightened but that he finally seemed to remember that his father was coming to a town called Integrity to be the town marshal."

"Well, then," Palmer said, "I guess I'd better go and find this Lieutenant Hendricks."

"He'll probably want to take you back to Fort Meade with him," the mayor said.

"I'll find out and let you know, Mr. Mayor."

"For your sake," Mayor O'Connor said, "I hope it's your boy."

Palmer got out of the office fast before the mayor could ask what the boy's name was.

CHAPTER TWENTY-SEVEN

PALMER FOUND THE lieutenant in the Palomino. His
men were at the bar and sitting at tables, but the
lieutenant was sitting alone.

Palmer went to the bar first.

"These soldiers are lookin' for you, Marshal," Wade
said, "especially that one sittin' over there."

"So I heard," Palmer said. "Let me have a beer and
I'll take it with me."

"Bring him a fresh one, too," Wade said, setting two
on the bar.

"Thanks, Wade."

Palmer picked up both beers and walked over to the
lieutenant's table.

"Lieutenant Hendricks?"

The man looked up, saw the badge on Palmer's
chest.

"Marshal Cassidy?" he said.

"That's right," Palmer said. "The bartender sent this over for you."

"I actually told my men they were only allowed one drink," the younger man said, "but what's the point of being in charge if you can't bend the rules for yourself? Thank you." He took the beer from Palmer. "Have a seat, Marshal."

Palmer sat across from the lieutenant.

"I assume you've already talked with your mayor."

"I have."

"Then you know why I'm here," Hendricks said. "We managed to rescue your son from the Sioux."

"A boy who might be my son," Palmer corrected.

"Well," Hendricks said, "that's something we won't know until you come to Fort Meade and identify him."

"That makes sense."

"We can leave as soon as we finish these beers. Unless you've got something more important to do?"

"What could be more important than identifying my son?" Palmer asked, because he thought that was what he'd be expected to say.

"Excellent!" Hendricks said. "We can make it back to Fort Meade before nightfall."

"Sounds good," Palmer said. "I'll have to go saddle my horse."

"Then we can meet right out front," Hendricks said.

Palmer drank half his beer down, then said, "I'll get right to it."

He left the saloon and headed for the livery, wondering if there was any way out of this.

*   *   *

PALMER DIDN'T COME up with anything, so ended up riding back to Fort Meade with Lieutenant Hendricks and his men.

Hendricks rode ahead of the column while Palmer hung back and rode alongside Corporal Agarn.

"Sounds like things got pretty exciting," he commented.

"Excitin'" ain't the word for it," Agarn said. He was an old-timer, a career soldier who never would rise above the rank of corporal.

"What do you mean?"

"Hendricks went off his rocker," Agarn said. "We didn't hafta ride in there with our guns blazin'. But his orders were to shoot to kill."

"Were there young warriors in that camp?"

"A few, but he wanted us to shoot anything that moved—anybody who wasn't white, that is." Agarn shook his head. "It was a bloodbath. Women, children, old men, it didn't matter."

"Is the lieutenant always that . . . bloodthirsty?" Palmer asked.

"He is," Agarn said. "But I shouldn't—"

He was cut off when the Irish sergeant came riding to join them.

"Agarn! Take up the rear!"

"Yes, Sergeant!"

Agarn turned his horse and rode away. Muldoon fell into place next to Palmer.

"What was he sayin'?" the soldier asked.

"We were just talking about the rescue," Palmer said.

"You shouldn't listen to anythin' he has to say."

"He just told me how bloody it got," Palmer said. "I'm glad the captives weren't hurt with all that lead flying around."

"They were all in a tepee, out of the line of fire," Muldoon said.

"I've never known a tepee that could keep a bullet out," Palmer said.

"We were careful," Muldoon said.

"Careful to shoot any Indian that moved?"

"Is that what Agarn told you?" Muldoon asked. "Look, we just followed orders."

"Orders that you agreed with?" Palmer asked.

"It ain't my job to agree or disagree," Muldoon said. "It's my job to follow orders."

"Even if they come from a young lieutenant who's not making any sense?"

"Look, I tried to tell 'im—" He stopped short.

"That it wasn't a good idea?"

"That we didn't have to go in hard like that," Muldoon said. "We had them outnumbered and we took 'em by surprise."

"Did you tell your commanding officer that?" Palmer asked.

"No," Muldoon said, "it ain't my way to go behind my lieutenant's back."

"So what are you going to do so it doesn't happen again?"

"I gotta keep tryin' to teach 'im," Muldoon said. "I got to get that West Point nonsense out of his head."

"And hope he doesn't kill too many more people," Palmer pointed out.

Muldoon gave Palmer a hard look.

"You think I should turn 'im in?"

"Look," Palmer said. "I don't know him. I don't know you or your CO, so I can't make a decision like that. You're the only one who has all the information."

"I just gotta do my job," Muldoon said. "The best thing for you to do is not talk to any more of my men."

"I understand."

Muldoon nodded and spurred his horse on ahead.

Palmer thought about seeking Agarn out again, but in the end, he decided to ride the rest of the way alone. He still had a lot of thinking to do.

WHEN THEY REACHED Fort Meade, the corporal took the column of soldiers off one way, while Lieutenant Hendricks and Sergeant Muldoon took Palmer to the commanding officer's office. They dismounted in front and a private came over to take their horses.

Inside, Lieutenant Hendricks went to the man seated at a desk and said, "Captain, this is Marshal Abe Cassidy from Integrity. The colonel is waiting to see him."

"Marshal," the captain said, standing. He was a slender man in his mid-thirties. "I'm Captain Enbrow, the colonel's adjutant. If you'll just wait a moment, I'll tell him you're here."

"Thank you."

Enbrow turned and knocked on his CO's door, then went in. Moments later he reappeared.

"The colonel will see you now, sir," he told Palmer.

"Thank you."

As Palmer started past the captain, the lieutenant tried to follow.

"Not you, Lieutenant," the captain said. "Just the marshal."

Hendricks looked shocked, but Muldoon smirked behind his back.

As Palmer entered, the CO stood up and came around the desk to shake his hand. He was about five feet eight or nine, in his sixties, with a head of shocking white hair with eyebrows to match.

"Marshal," he said, "I'm happy to meet you. I'm Colonel Harold Stockton."

"Colonel."

They shook hands and the colonel said, "Please, have a seat."

The CO went back around behind his desk and the two men sat facing each other.

"I hope we haven't made you ride out here for nothing," Stockton said. "It took our doctor a while to get the boy to talk. Apparently, he'd been with the Sioux for six months."

"Have they mistreated him?" Palmer asked.

"Our doctor said that he and the other captives are healthy," Stockton said. "It looks like they've been fed, but all of the kids we rescued were very frightened when we brought them here. Some of them had been with the Sioux for a few years, and we haven't found their parents. A couple of the others were there for a couple of months, and we've managed to send them back home. Now all that remains is your boy."

"If he's my boy," Palmer said.

"Exactly. And whenever you're ready, we'll go over to the infirmary and have a look."

Palmer knew if this was, indeed, the son of Abraham Cassidy, his time as marshal of Integrity would probably be over. All he had to do was walk over to the infirmary and be exposed. He couldn't think of anything else to do but get it over with.

"Why don't we do that?" Palmer asked. "Will your lieutenant and sergeant be coming with us?"

"Hendricks and Muldoon?" the colonel said. "Do you want them to?"

"No."

"That was quite definitive," Stockton said. "May I ask why not?"

"I'm afraid they'll scare the boy," Palmer said. "I heard it was a real bloodbath out there. I also heard the boy got hit on the head. I'm hoping he's all right and he'll recognize me after six months. But I think it would be better with fewer people around, especially soldiers."

"Very well," the colonel said, "but I'll need to come along."

"That's okay," Palmer said. "If you don't mind me saying so, there's nothing frightening about you."

The colonel stood up and straightened his tunic. He grabbed his hat, strapped on his saber, and said, "Let's take that walk."

When they left the office, Lieutenant Hendricks started talking right away.

"Colonel, I think I should tell you—"

"Save it, Lieutenant," Stockton said. "Marshal Cassidy and I are walking over to the infirmary."

"Good," Hendricks said, "but I think I should come alon—"

"You and Sergeant Muldoon will wait right here," Stockton told them.

Sergeant Muldoon gave Palmer a look that said he knew the lawman had said something to the CO.

"Sir," Hendricks went on, "I think—"

"I think you'd better stand down, Lieutenant," Captain Enbrow said.

Hendricks looked at the captain, then at the colonel, a helpless expression on his face, and finally glanced at Sergeant Muldoon, who looked away.

"After you, Marshal," the colonel said.

Palmer and Stockton left the office and started walking across the compound.

"Tell me, Marshal," the old soldier said, "why do I feel you know something that I don't know?"

"I can't imagine, sir," Palmer said. "Right now I'm just concerned with seeing the boy."

"Of course," Stockton said, "but we're going to talk more."

When they reached the infirmary, the colonel opened the door and allowed Palmer to precede him. A man wearing a white coat over a uniform turned to face them. He was in his forties, with steel-gray hair.

"Marshal, this is our doctor, Captain Torrence."

Palmer shook the man's hand.

"He's here to see the boy," Stockton said.

"Of course," Torrence said. "I'll bring him right out." He went into another room.

This was the moment. Palmer was thinking the best thing for him to do was probably to have left town and not ridden out to Fort Meade. How was he going to brazen this out when the boy looked at him and said he was not his father? His only hope was that the boy might be addled by his experience.

The doctor returned with a small, thin boy who Palmer had been told was eleven or twelve but looked younger. The boy moved stiffly, walking with his hands at his sides and his head down. His hair was chopped short. It probably had been long when they brought him in.

"Jeffrey," the doctor said, "say hello to your father."

The boy's head came up, his eyes locked on Palmer's face for a moment, then widened.

Palmer was shocked when the boy shouted, "Pa!" and ran to wrap his arms around his waist.

CHAPTER TWENTY-EIGHT

P A! OH, PA!" the boy said, holding on tight.

Palmer was stunned and tried not to show it.

"Easy, boy," he said. "You're safe now."

Palmer looked down at the boy. Then, when he looked up, he saw Colonel Stockton and the doctor watching him.

"I don't know how to thank you," he said.

"So this is your boy?" the colonel said.

"Yes," Palmer said, "yes, this is Jeff—yes, it's him."

Both men stared at him a little longer, then smiled.

"Then you should take your son home, Marshal," Stockton said. "I'll just need you to come back to my office and sign some papers."

Palmer held the boy at arm's length, saw the anxious look on his face.

"Don't worry, Jeffrey," he said. "You're safe now."

The doctor came forward and put his hands on the boy's thin shoulders.

"I'll get him cleaned up and dressed to travel," he offered.

Palmer realized the boy was wearing some sort of nightshirt.

"Good idea, Doc," he said.

"Come on, Jeffrey," Doc Torrence said.

The boy was afraid to let go of Palmer.

"It's all right," Palmer said. "Go with the doctor. I'll be back here to fetch you in a few minutes."

Reluctantly, the boy allowed the doctor to tug him away.

"Let's go back to my office and get this done," Stockton said.

When they returned, they found the lieutenant and the sergeant still there.

"How did it go, sir?" Captain Enbrow asked.

"It's his boy, all right," Stockton said. "He'll be taking him home. Get me the proper paperwork, Captain."

"Yes, sir."

"You two," Stockton said to the other men, "remain here until I come out."

"Yes, sir," Hendricks said.

Stockton and Palmer went into his office. The colonel sat behind his desk and looked up at Palmer.

"Now, Marshal," Stockton said, "tell me what you heard about this bloodbath."

WHEN THE OFFICE door opened again, Lieutenant Hendricks looked up impatiently.

Captain Enbrow came out and sat back down at his desk.

"How much longer, Captain?" Hendricks asked.

"I don't know, Lieutenant," the captain said. "I don't ask the colonel those kinds of questions."

"Easy, lad," Sergeant Muldoon said.

"Don't talk to me like that, Sergeant," Hendricks said.

"I'm just tryin' to keep you from makin' a mistake, Lieutenant. It's my job."

"To look after me?"

"That's right."

"Who says so?"

"The Army," Muldoon said. "They think you can learn from my experience."

"I went to West Point, Sergeant," the lieutenant said.

"I know," Muldoon said. "That's too bad."

Hendricks turned to say something sharp to the sergeant, but the colonel's door opened and he stopped.

"Captain, would you take the marshal over to the doctor to pick up his son, please."

"Yes, sir," the captain said, standing.

"Sergeant," Stockton said, "come in, please."

"Colonel," Lieutenant Hendricks said, "what about me?"

"You're next, Lieutenant," the colonel said, "have no doubt."

Muldoon walked into the colonel's office. The CO sat behind his desk and looked at him.

"Now tell me what happened," Stockton said, "and don't leave anything out."

* * *

PALMER FOLLOWED THE captain to the doctor's office, and then outside, he told the man, "I can take it from here."

"I'll have your horse brought over," the captain said, "and a horse for the boy."

"Thanks."

Palmer went into the doctor's barracks. Torrence and Jeffrey were standing there as if they had been waiting that way the whole time. The boy was wearing clothes that were too large for him, including a coat.

"Here's your pa, Jeffrey," the doctor said. "I hope everything will be all right for you now."

"Thank you, Doc," Palmer said. "Jeff?"

The boy walked toward him.

"Yes, Pa?"

"Are you ready to go?"

"Yes, Pa."

Palmer put his arm around the boy's thin shoulders and walked him outside. Right at that moment, a soldier was bringing two horses over to them.

"Can you ride?" Palmer asked.

"Yes."

"Let's go, then."

Palmer helped the boy into his saddle, where he sat uncomfortably. Living with the Sioux, he had probably ridden bareback.

Palmer mounted up and together they left Fort Meade.

Colonel Stockton had offered to put them up for the night, but Palmer had said he'd rather get started and camp with the boy under the stars. He said it might make the boy more comfortable, but the real reason was he wanted to get away from the fort before more questions were asked.

He and the boy didn't talk while they rode. When they made camp, Palmer told the boy to relax while he made a fire and tended to the horses. He had coffee and beef jerky in his saddlebags. He had some jerky with the coffee and gave Jeff some with water.

They sat across the fire from each other, and the boy stared at him. When he finally spoke, he asked, "Who are you?"

"My name's Marshal Abe Cassidy."

"No, it ain't," Jeffrey said. "You ain't my pa. My pa's dead, like my ma, my brothers, and my sisters. I saw them get killed."

"Why didn't you tell the Army I wasn't your pa?" Palmer asked.

"I didn't wanna stay there no more," the boy said. "And if I didn't say you was my pa, they'd have kept me a little longer and then sent me away."

"Where?"

The boy shrugged.

"Maybe a reservation. That's where they sent some of the others when they couldn't find their pa and ma."

"But you're not Sioux."

"That don't matter," the boy said. "To them I'm more Sioux than white."

"So you'd rather say I was your pa and leave with me," Palmer said.

"You don't gotta keep me," Jeffrey said. "I can go my own way in the morning. The Sioux taught me how to live."

"How old are you?"

"Twelve."

"You can't live on your own."

"You ain't my pa."

"I don't have to be your pa to take care of you," Palmer said, surprised to hear the words coming out of his mouth.

The truth of the matter was, it would cement his position in Integrity even more if he returned with the boy. He could have gone back and simply said that when he got to the fort, he saw the boy wasn't his son. But the mayor—and the town—would be happier if he returned with a son.

"Why are you usin' my pa's name?" Jeffrey asked.

"It's complicated."

The boy got a stubborn look on his face.

"I found them," Palmer said finally, "all dead, and I buried them. I was trying to leave my life behind, and I read your father's letters. It seemed like a good idea at the time. Leave myself behind and become Abraham Cassidy. There didn't seem to be any harm." Palmer leaned forward. "I thought your whole family was dead."

The boy thought about the story for a while, then looked across the fire at Palmer.

"You buried them all?"

"I did."

"Thank you."

"Will you come back to Integrity with me?" he asked. "It's where you were supposed to live."

"Where will I live?"

"With me," Palmer said. "You'll have to say that you're my son."

"And will I be your son?" Jeffrey asked.

"I don't know much about being a father," Palmer said, "so you'll have to teach me."

After a moment's hesitation, Jeffrey said, "All right."

"Did the Sioux give you an Indian name?"

"They called me Sharp Eagle."

"You'll have to go back to being Jeffrey Cassidy."

The boy smiled.

"I can do that . . . Pa."

DURING THE NIGHT Palmer became aware of the boy crying, wrapped in his blanket. He was obviously mourning his family, and Palmer decided just to let him have his private time. He probably had to mourn in order to move ahead with their plan to ride into Integrity as father and son. It couldn't have been an easy decision for the boy, even given what the alternatives were.

In the morning, they had jerky and coffee. Palmer gave the boy a cup to warm his belly. They then broke camp, saddled their horses, and headed for Integrity to start their new life as father and son.

CHAPTER TWENTY-NINE

Three years later . . .

Belle! what do I do with these?"
Belle Henderson turned and looked at Jeffrey Cassidy. Since the fifteen-year-old had started to work in her store several months earlier, things had been so much easier. She was lucky that after his most recent birthday, he had decided to get a job so he could start making his own money.

When Marshal Abe Cassidy had returned from Fort Meade with the son he thought was dead, he seemed like a much happier man. And the people in town were happy for him. Now that he had been the law in town for more than three years, he was totally entrenched and accepted in Integrity.

He and his son were also often guests of Belle's for supper. She enjoyed cooking for two hungry males.

"Put them on that top shelf, Jeffrey. Thank you."

"Yes, ma'am."

"Is your father coming back to town today?"

"Yes, ma'am. He said he was gonna deliver his prisoner to Pierre and then come right back."

Pierre was a town smack in the middle of the South Dakota Territory, across from Fort Pierre on the banks of the Missouri River. Jeffrey had wanted to go with Palmer—his "pa"—but the marshal had said no.

"It's going to be a quick trip," Palmer told the boy. "I need you to stay here and watch over Deputy Steve. You're also going to start working in Belle's store. You can't be taking time off already. Understand?"

"Yes, Pa."

Belle had been there when Palmer explained all this to the boy, and she decided not to make any remarks. This was between father and son. Besides, she did need help in the store, which was becoming busier as the town grew.

After the boy finished stacking items on the top shelf, Belle said, "Jeffrey, why don't you go in the back and make some room for our next delivery?"

"Yes, ma'am."

"After that, we'll get some lunch."

As Jeffrey went into the storeroom, the front door opened and Mayor O'Connor entered the store. He was in the midst of his second term of office, and one of the things that had gotten him reelected turned out to be bringing Marshal Abraham Cassidy to town.

"Mr. Mayor," Belle greeted, "what can we do for you today, sir?"

"Nothing too important, Mrs. Henderson," O'Connor said. "I just need some of my pipe tobacco."

"Of course, sir," she said. "We have it right here. How many packs?"

"Two, I think."

"Here you go."

"Thank you." O'Connor had made the purchase enough times to know the cost already, so he passed her the money. "How's your new employee doing?"

"Jeffrey is wonderful," she said. "He's just tall enough to be a big help with the top shelves."

"He seems to be a fine boy," O'Connor said. "Being rescued and reunited with his father seems to have changed both of their lives."

"The marshal's always been a good man," Belle said. "But I agree with you. Gettin' his son back seemed to make him more . . . approachable."

"Well, he certainly has settled into the job," O'Connor said, "and I've got to admit, he did all right hiring a deputy. Steve Atlee would not have been my first choice, but he seems to be doing the job. Yes, sir, we've been lucky to have had three-and-a-half solid years of law enforcement in Integrity."

"And I'm sure we'll have many more," Belle said.

O'CONNOR LEFT THE mercantile, amazed at Belle Henderson's attitude, since the last incident of violence in town had been the unexpected shootings of her husband and her.

She'd managed to retain ownership of the store, which appeared to be prospering, and folks in town seemed to think that she and the marshal were headed for the altar soon.

He stopped walking when he saw three strangers riding into town. Integrity was still off the beaten path, but it was growing, and strangers in town were always welcome. But these looked like saddle tramps, and O'Connor wasn't happy to see them with Marshal Cassidy away. He decided to make a stop in the marshal's office. Steve Atlee might not have been his first choice as deputy, but he was the deputy the town had.

D EPUTY ATLEE WAS pouring himself a cup of coffee when the office door opened and Mayor O'Connor stepped in. Atlee knew the mayor didn't want him to be a deputy, but Marshal Cassidy had made the decision. But after all these years, he still felt as if the mayor didn't approve.

"Mr. Mayor," he said, "what can I do for you?"

"I understand we're expecting the marshal back today," O'Connor said.

"That's right," Atlee said, "later today." He carried his coffee to the desk and sat. There was still only one desk in the room, but that was all they needed. A second one would have made the area look and feel crowded. What they really needed was a new office.

"Well," O'Connor said, "I wanted you to know I just saw three strangers ride into town."

"That right?" Atlee asked. "What'd they look like?"

"Like saddle tramps on horseback," O'Connor said. "In fact, you might even say they looked like hard cases."

"Maybe I should take a look at them," the deputy said.

"You probably should," O'Connor said, "but I wouldn't approach them. Not till the marshal gets back."

"I'd only talk to them, Mr. Mayor."

"Who knows who they are, if they're wanted somewhere or not?" the mayor said. "And if push came to shove, it would be three against one. No, I just want you to take a look at them and know where they are for when the marshal gets back."

"Okay," Atlee said, "I can do that."

"Excellent," the mayor said. "Thank you, Deputy."

"You didn't happen to see what hotel they went to, did you?" Atlee asked.

"I don't even know if they stopped at a hotel, the livery, or a saloon."

Over the past three years, another hotel and two more saloons had opened in town. Atlee figured he'd have to check all of them.

"All right, Mr. Mayor," he said. "Thanks for lettin' me know."

"Just remember to be careful, Deputy," O'Connor said.

"Yes, sir," Atlee said, "I'll do that."

The mayor nodded and left the office.

Atlee sipped his coffee. He had planned to sweep the office so it looked clean when the marshal arrived, but now he was thinking he had something else to occupy his time. He set his cup down, put on his hat, and left the office.

I N ADDITION TO the Palomino, the Last Chance, the Little Dakota, and the Silver Spur saloons, the town now also had the Diamond Lady and Bill Dunlap's Saloon. As for hotels, the Utopia had put Integrity's other hotel out of business the first year it was open, but since then another had opened called Integrity House. So Atlee had eight places to check—not to mention the two hotels had their own saloons for their guests—but even before that, he went to the livery stable to see if three strangers had boarded their horses.

"No strangers today, Deputy," the hostler, Lionel, told him. "Sorry."

Atlee thanked the man, then went to the hotels to talk to the desk clerks. The word was the same there: no strangers.

After that, Atlee went saloon crawling. There were horses outside most of them, but it was still early in the day and none of them was busy. He approached each bartender and asked about strangers. Finally, at the fourth place he tried—the new Diamond Lady Saloon— he got the word.

"Well, yeah, Deputy," the barkeep said. "Three strangers came in a little while ago. They ordered a bottle of whiskey and three glasses and went to a back table."

"Don't point," Atlee said. "Just tell me where."

"Under the painting of the Diamond Lady where she's wearin' green."

There were several paintings of the Diamond Lady on the walls, all in different color dresses. Atlee turned his head and glanced at the three men seated beneath the green one. The mayor had been right. They looked like hard cases.

"No trouble?" he asked the bartender.

"Not yet."

"They didn't happen to say what they were doin' here, did they?"

"No, sir."

"Okay, thanks," Atlee said.

"You gonna ask 'em?" the bartender asked.

"Not just yet."

Atlee turned from the bar, made a point of not looking at the three men again, and left.

SEE?" RUSTY BRIGGS said. "I tol' you. I ain't wanted here, so there's no reason for the law to look at us twice."

"Except that we're strangers," Johnny Brickhill said.

"And we look like saddle tramps," Chad Green said, rubbing his face, "what with this beard stubble and these dirty clothes."

"We can fix that," Briggs said, "with a bath and some new clothes."

"A bath?" Green said, almost in shock.

"Hey, you're the one who talked about us bein' dirty," Briggs said. "We can probably use a haircut as well as a shave."

"You sure you ain't wanted here?" Brickhill asked.

"All through the Southwest, yeah," Briggs said, "but ain't no paper out on me up here. That's for sure."

"Well, then," Green said, grabbing the bottle, "we got time to have a few more drinks."

"Just remember," Briggs said. "If we split up, no trouble. We don't wanna attract any attention. Got it?"

"We got it," Brickhill said. "I just got one question."

"What's that?"

"How long we gotta stay up here?"

"Until I figure out some way to make money," Briggs told him. "Pour me another drink."

CHAPTER THIRTY

PALMER RODE BACK into Integrity around supper-time. That meant the street wasn't busy, businesses were closed or closing, and he was hungry. While he had been away for a few days, he had camped out a couple of times, and he was feeling grimy. He had more beard stubble on his face than he'd had since coming to town over three years ago. He was longing for a hot bath and some fresh clothes. But he stopped first at his office, even before taking his horse to the livery.

"Marshal!" Steve Atlee said as he entered. "Glad to see you back."

"Happy to be back, Steve," Palmer said. "Anything happen while I was away?"

"Not a thing," Atlee said. "Oh, some strangers rode in today, and the mayor was kinda worried, but I took a look at 'em."

"And?"

"They look like hard cases, but they didn't match any posters that we've got," Atlee said. "And all they was doin' when I saw them was sittin' and drinkin'."

"You get any names?"

"Nope."

"Know if they're staying or just passing through?" Palmer asked.

"No."

"What *did* you find out, Steve?" Palmer asked.

"Just that they're here," Atlee said, "and so far there's been no trouble."

"And they got here today, you said?"

"Yes, sir."

"Okay." Palmer rubbed his face. "I'm too tired to deal with them now. I need a bath, a meal, and some sleep. I'll check in on them tomorrow."

"Whatever you say, Marshal."

Palmer wished Atlee had been a little more thorough in investigating the three strangers. Then again, he would have been one man against three, which wasn't smart, especially if they were gunnies. Better to wait till tomorrow and brace them together.

"Okay," Palmer said, "I'm going to tend to my horse, then go home, see if I can find my son, and get settled."

"He's been working for Miss Belle at her store," Atlee said. "I saw him there earlier today."

"That's right," Palmer said. "She gave him a job, didn't she? But she'd probably be closed by now. I'll check and see if he's home. I won't be back tonight, Steve, so you close the office, and then I'll open it up in the morning."

"Suits me, boss," Atlee said.

Palmer left the office and rode his horse over to the livery stable.

"Welcome back, Marshal," the hostler, Lionel, said, taking his horse from him. "I was gonna stop by your office after I closed up."

"What for?"

"Your deputy was here earlier today askin' me about strangers."

"And?"

"I hadn't seen any, but since then a man came in leading three horses, said he'd just gotten to town."

"Three horses?"

"That's right."

"Where are they?"

"My three back stalls. I'll show you."

The older man walked Palmer back, showed him the three animals. Two were geldings and one a mare. They all looked to be seven or eight years old and well traveled.

"They've come a long way," Palmer said.

"From the Southwest, the man said," the hostler told him. "He was a talker."

"Did he say why they were here?"

"No, but he did say they'd be at the Integrity House, probably for a few days, and that they'd probably want to buy some horses when they're ready to leave."

"Are their saddles here?"

"Yeah, over there."

Palmer went to the three saddles and saw that all three saddlebags were gone.

"There's nothing here to tell me anything," he said.

"Well, you're the marshal," the hostler said. "You can just ask 'em what they're doin' here."

"And I will," Palmer said. "Tomorrow."

Palmer left the livery and started walking home. After he had returned from Fort Meade with the boy, he had moved out of the hotel and into the house the town was originally going to give Abe Cassidy. It was still a little large for him and the boy, but they made it home, furnishing it with the help of Belle Henderson.

Now that Jeffrey was fifteen, Palmer had agreed to leave him home on his own while he took the prisoner to Pierre. In the past when he'd had to leave town, he would have left the boy with Belle, but Jeffrey insisted he was old enough to look after himself. What he didn't know was that when Palmer had agreed, he'd also asked Belle to look in on Jeffrey.

As Palmer entered the large one-story house on the southern edge of town, Jeffrey came out of the kitchen, chewing on a chicken leg.

"Belle sent us some cold chicken," he said with a smile.

"And you couldn't wait for me to get home to eat it?" Palmer asked.

The broad smile became a sheepish one.

"I was hungry, and you said you'd probably be home by this time."

"Lucky for me I was right," Palmer said, "or you might have eaten all that chicken yourself."

They went into the kitchen together, and while Palmer washed up in the sink, Jeffrey laid out plates for the chicken. Palmer dried his hands and sat at the table with his "son."

He had to admit, after living with the boy for three years and watching him mature and grow, he did love him like a son. It was a feeling he never would have thought he was capable of as Tom Palmer. But as Abe Cassidy, he was a doting father.

And even though Jeffrey knew Palmer was not his real father, he had kept his word and stayed silent, for he would always appreciate Palmer for stopping to bury his family. In the end, Palmer's taking Jeffrey's father's name and identity had helped the both of them.

"Any trouble with the prisoner?" Jeffrey asked.

"None," Palmer said. "I took him there, turned him over, and headed home."

"And you didn't have a beer first?"

"One."

"Ha!"

Palmer stared across the table at Jeffrey. He looked quite different from the skinny boy Palmer had brought back from Fort Meade that day. He had grown a head taller, filled out so that he almost looked like a full-grown man. Three years ago he had fought the idea of a haircut, but had finally given in and let a barber cut off those long Indian-like locks. When Jeffrey had some new clothes, it turned out he looked just like every other kid in town, and nobody looked at him twice. Palmer put him in school and nobody teased the marshal's son about having lived with the Sioux for six months.

When they finished eating, Jeffrey volunteered to wash the dishes.

"What have you done with my son?" Palmer asked.

"You look tired," Jeffrey said. "Why don't you just go to sleep?"

"It'll be nice to be in my own bed," Palmer admitted.

"Then in the morning you can take a bath," the boy added. "You stink."

CHAPTER THIRTY-ONE

PALMER AND JEFFREY did not have a bathtub in their house, so Palmer rose early and went into town to bathe. While he did that, Jeffrey went to the mercantile store to help Belle.

Palmer intended to also have a shave and a haircut, but the barber had somebody in his chair, and two more people waiting, so Palmer decided to return later.

Across from the barber was a small hotel that hadn't been there when Palmer first came to town. It was probably the cheaper of the two hotels in town to stay in. There was a man out front lighting a cigarette when Palmer came out of the barbershop. As the marshal headed off down the street, the man with the cigarette stared so long, the match burned down to his fingers.

"Sonofabitch!" he swore for two reasons.

* * *

W HO?" RUSTY BRIGGS asked.
          "Tommy Palmer," Johnny Brickhill said.
"Come on, you've heard of him. He's wanted in as
many places as you are."

"And he's here?"

Brickhill nodded.

"I just saw him comin' out of the barbershop."

"And you're sure it's him?" Briggs asked.

"I know 'im, Rusty," Brickhill said. "We pulled a
few jobs together. He's shaved off his beard, but he has
enough stubble on his face that I still recognized him."

"But he was comin' out of a barbershop," Chad
Green said. "He didn't have a shave?"

"I looked in the window after he left. There were
some fellas in there waitin'. I guessed he was gonna
come back, but I went inside to ask."

"And?" Briggs said.

"The barber told me it was the marshal, Abe Cassidy, and that he'd be back later for a haircut and a
shave. Apparently, he just got back from transportin' a
prisoner."

The three of them were sitting in the Little Dakota
Saloon with beers in front of them.

"So this Marshal Cassidy looks like your Tommy
Palmer?" Briggs said.

"No," Brickhill said, "he don't look like him. It's
him. He walks like him and wears his gun like him."

"So what's he doin' livin' here as a town marshal?"
Briggs asked.

"Well, like I said," Brickhill answered, "he's wanted

in as many places as you are. I guess he came up here to hide out and took the marshal's job under another name."

"So he switched sides," Chad Green said. "He's on the wrong side of the law now."

"I guess that depends on how you look at it," Brickhill said.

"So what do you wanna do?" Briggs asked.

"I don't know," Brickhill said. "Now that he's back in town, I guess we're gonna run into him. Unless we leave."

"I'm not ready to leave yet," Briggs said.

"Well, then, I guess I can just pretend I didn't recognize him."

"I've got a better idea," Briggs said.

"What's that?"

"How much is the price on his head?" Briggs asked.

"At least as much as yours," Brickhill said.

"Five thousand?"

"In some places."

"Well," Briggs said, "that's certainly an amount of money we could use."

Brickhill looked surprised.

"You want to turn him in for the reward?" he asked. "How you gonna do that without turnin' yourself in, too?"

"I'm not gonna turn him in for the reward," Briggs said. "You are."

TWO HOURS LATER, Palmer came out of the barbershop, shorn and shaved.

"Well, I'll be—" a voice said.

Palmer turned and saw the man who had spoken. After more than three years in Integrity, and at the point where he was firmly entrenched there as Marshal Cassidy, here was a face he recognized and one that apparently recognized him.

He decided to try to brazen it out.

"What's that?" he asked.

"Tommy, come on," the man said. "It's me, Johnny Brickhill."

"Oh," Palmer said, "you must be one of the three strangers who rode into town yesterday."

"That's right."

"I was going to come over and talk to you fellas," Palmer said.

"With that badge on and your beard gone, I almost didn't recognize you, Tommy," Brickhill said. "But I saw you goin' into the barbershop with enough stubble on your face for me to know it was you."

Damn, Palmer thought. He should have gotten that shave as soon as he returned to town. That was careless.

"Come on, Tommy," Brickhill said, "it's me. It's Brick. Whataya doin' up here with that badge on? Do they know who you are?"

Palmer realized there was no getting rid of Johnny Brickhill.

"Come to my office with me," he said. "We can talk there."

"Sure, Tommy, sure."

"And don't call me Tommy!" Palmer hissed.

He led the way to his office. As they entered, Steve Atlee looked up from the desk.

"Make some rounds, Steve."

"I did my rounds, Marshal—"

"Do them again!" Palmer snapped. Then added, "Please."

"Okay," Atlee said, "sure, Marshal."

He grabbed his hat, gave Palmer and the other man a puzzled look, and left.

"Have a seat, Brick."

"So it is you," Brickhill said, sitting. "You ain't denyin' it?"

"Would it do any good?"

"No," Brickhill said. "I knew it was you. Whataya doin' up here, Tommy? And what name are you usin'?"

"I'm not wanted up here," Palmer said. "And I wanted to stop running, at least for a while. When I realized this job was open, I thought I'd grab it."

"How did you manage that?"

Palmer wondered if he should tell the truth or lie, but he'd already been caught, so he told Brickhill the whole story.

"Wow," the man said. "You know, the times we worked together I knew you were smart. But this . . . What's your name?"

"Cassidy," Palmer said, "Marshal Abraham Cassidy."

"Marshal Cassidy," Brickhill repeated. "Not bad. You know, there's still paper out on you in the Southwest."

"I figured," Palmer said. "Those things don't go away."

"You ever gonna go back south?"

"I don't see why," Palmer said, "unless you're going to go back and tell the law I'm here?"

"What good would that do?" Brickhill said. "They can't come here and get you unless they get a federal warrant issued."

"And they'd do that only if somebody told them I was here," Palmer pointed out. "You going to do that, Brick?"

"Me?" Brickhill said. "Tom—Marshal, we're friends, ain't we?"

Palmer had never thought of any of the men he'd pulled jobs with as friends. He never understood why or how a dishonest man would honor a friendship.

"By the way," he asked, "who're you here with?"

"Two fellas named Rusty Briggs and Chad Green," Brickhill said.

"Wanted?"

"Briggs is," Brickhill said. "He's got about as much paper out on him as you do. Me and Chad, we're small potatoes. No posters."

"Lucky you."

"You know," Brickhill said, "if I'd seen you only with this haircut and shave, I don't know if I woulda recognized you."

"I figured."

"That was pretty careless of you."

"Yeah," Palmer said, "I think I got too comfortable thinking nobody I know would end up here."

"You're gonna have to be more careful in the future, Marshal," Brickhill said, standing up. "I'm guessin' you won't wanna have a drink with me while I'm here."

"I'm thinking that wouldn't be a good idea, Brick," Palmer said.

"I getcha, Marshal, I getcha," Brickhill said. "If I see ya around town, I won't let on."

"I appreciate that, Brick," Palmer said.

Brickhill nodded, touched the brim of his hat, and left the office.

CHAPTER THIRTY-TWO

AFTER JOHNNY BRICKHILL left the office, Palmer sat there at his desk and did some quick thinking. Probably the best solution to the problem was to kill Brickhill. The only problem with that was Tom Palmer had been an outlaw for most of his life since he was sixteen years old, but not a killer. And there were two other men with Brickhill. Palmer didn't bother asking if Brickhill was going to tell his partners about the town marshal being an old comrade in arms. Brick probably would've lied and said no.

Palmer decided he was just going to have to wait and see if Brickhill returned to the Southwest and gave him up. Still, he doubted even in that case that a federal warrant would be issued. But you never knew what a bounty hunter would do. Palmer was going to have to go back to being very careful.

And he still had Jeffrey to consider. . . .

* * *

BRICKHILL FOUND BRIGGS and Green right where he left them, in the Little Dakota. It was early, but the grubby little saloon was open. He sat down in front of the beer they had waiting on the table for him.

"So?" Briggs asked as Brickhill sat.

"It's him."

"He admits it?"

"Yup."

"What's he doin' up here?"

"Hidin'," Brickhill said. "Livin' under somebody else's name."

"I gotta admit," Briggs said, "that's pretty smart."

"So whatta we do now?" Chad Green asked.

"That's easy," Briggs said. "We take him back to wherever he's wanted—"

"New Mexico, Texas, Arizona," Brickhill said. "You name it."

"—and turn him over for the reward."

"And then?" Green asked.

"And then we split it three ways."

Brickhill was quiet.

"Whatsamatta, Brick?" Green asked.

"Feelin' guilty about turnin' in a friend?" Briggs asked.

"We was never exactly friends," Brickhill admitted. "We pulled some jobs together over the years, is all."

"So whataya feelin'?" Briggs asked.

"I dunno," Brickhill said. "It ain't guilt exactly. It's . . . I dunno. It just don't feel . . . right."

"You said the price on his head is as big as mine," Briggs said.

"That's right."

"Well, I know in Texas they got five thousand on my head," Briggs said. "Is that enough to make it feel right for you?"

Brickhill thought the question over, picked up his beer, and said, "Yeah, I guess so."

"Okay." Briggs and Green picked up their beers as well. "This is how we'll do it. . . ."

PALMER STOPPED IN at the mercantile to see Jeffrey and Belle.

"Ah, you're back," Belle said.

"Got in yesterday."

"And you're only comin' to see me now?" she asked. He smiled.

"I needed to get cleaned up first," he said.

"I can see that," she said. "Haircut and a close, close shave. Looks good."

"Where's Jeff?" he asked.

"I've got him doin' some work in the storeroom." She frowned. "Anythin' wrong?"

"Not really," he said. "I just need to talk to him."

"Well, go on back, then," she said. "I'll stay here and give you some privacy."

"Thanks."

As he walked to the back, she called out, "Just don't talk about me."

Palmer went through the curtained doorway, saw Jeffrey stacking boxes. The boy was almost six feet tall and had filled out. He bore no resemblance to the kid who had been rescued from the Sioux three years ago.

"You here to help me?" Jeff asked when he saw Palmer.

"Not exactly, but I don't see why I can't while I'm here."

"Good," Jeff said. "Help me with this crate. It's heavy."

Palmer went over and together they moved the heavy crate across the room.

"Thanks," Jeff said, pausing to rest. "What brings you here?"

"I have to tell you something," Palmer said. He had decided to keep the boy informed no matter what happened. After all, he was the only one in town who knew the truth.

"Sounds serious."

"It might be. Sit down a minute."

They each chose a crate to sit on and Palmer told Jeffrey what the problem was.

"Is he gonna tell anybody?" Jeffrey asked when Palmer finished. "Like the mayor?"

"He says no."

"Do you believe him?"

"I don't know," Palmer said. "I think we're just going to have to be ready for whatever happens, Jeff."

Jeffrey stood up in front of Palmer.

"Why don't we just leave?"

"What?"

"Yeah," the boy said, "you and me, let's get out before this Brick and his friends ruin everythin'."

"Easy, Jeff," Palmer said. "Let's not go off half-cocked. Brick and his friends may just leave town. Let's wait and see."

Jeffrey sat back down.

"You know," he said, "I'm almost sixteen."

"In six more months," Palmer said. "What's your point?"

"You told me you pulled your first job at sixteen," Jeffrey said. "If I knew how to handle a gun, I could back you up."

"I have a deputy for that."

"No," Jeffrey said, "I mean back up the real you."

"Jeff," Palmer said, "when you're sixteen, I'll teach you to shoot. Not before." Palmer stood up. "You'd better get back to work."

"And you'd better be careful," Jeff said, then added, "Pa."

Palmer went back to the front of the store.

"Trouble?" Belle asked.

"There might be," Palmer said. "There are three strangers in town I may have to deal with."

"Why don't you and Jeff come to supper tonight?" Belle suggested. "You can tell me all about it then. Or not."

"That sounds like a good idea," Palmer said. "You take him home from here with you, and I'll be there later."

"Where are you off to now?" she asked.

"Just to do my job," Palmer said.

S o?" CHAD GREEN asked. "Do we go and get him now?"

"Just relax," Briggs said. "He's the law. He'll be comin' to us."

"You sure about that?" Brickhill asked.

"I know lawmen, Brick," Briggs said. "He'll be comin' to take a look at Chad and me."

CHAPTER THIRTY-THREE

PALMER LEFT THE mercantile and decided to check the saloons. Knowing that the two other strangers in town were with Johnny Brickhill, he decided to check the worst saloon first. That was the Little Dakota.

As he reached the saloon, he peered in over the bat-wing doors. He spotted Johnny Brickhill seated at a table with two other men. There were no other customers, so the only other person in the place was the bartender.

Palmer entered the saloon, drawing the attention of all four men.

"Marshal," Brickhill said, "lookin' for me?"

"For the three of you, actually," Palmer said, approaching the table. "I thought maybe you'd introduce me to your friends."

"Really?" Brickhill asked. "Under which name?"

Palmer looked at the other two men, who were staring at him.

"I'll bet you already told them," he said.

"Well," Brickhill said, "we're partners."

"Have a seat, Marshal," Briggs said. "Is there somethin' on your mind?"

Palmer didn't sit.

"I was just wondering how long you fellas plan on being here in town?" Palmer said.

"Well," Briggs said, "we really hadn't intended to come here, at all. None of us had ever heard of Integrity before."

"So if you didn't plan to stop here, you have no plan about when you leave."

"That's pretty much it, uh, Marshal," Briggs said.

"I understand none of you is wanted up here," Palmer said. "Are you going to keep it that way?"

"I have no plans to break the law hereabouts, Marshal," Briggs said. "Do you?"

"I wouldn't break the law since I *am* the law," Palmer said.

"That's what everybody around here thinks, isn't it?" Briggs asked.

Palmer stared at him.

"Oh, don't worry, Marshal," Briggs said, laughing. "We're not gonna open our mouths. Your secret is safe with us." He looked over at the bar. "Even the bartender doesn't know what we're talkin' about."

"Still," Palmer said, "I think it would be better if the three of you left town tomorrow. Better for all of us."

With that, Palmer turned and left the saloon.

"Chad," Rusty Briggs said, "get three more beers. We got a plan to make."

B Y THE TIME they finished their beers, the plan was set.

"Why didn't we grab him while he was here?" Chad Green asked.

"Because I didn't want to have to kill the bartender," Briggs said. "We don't need no witnesses."

"He's got a deputy," Brickhill said.

"We'll go around him," Briggs said. "We'll grab Palmer off the street when he's alone and then light out. We head south and keep goin' until we can turn 'im in."

"You'll want one of us to do it," Brickhill said. "You don't wanna take a chance on bein' recognized yourself."

"You got that right."

"I don't wanna do it," Green said.

Briggs and Brickhill both looked at the younger man.

"I'd feel like I'm turnin' one of our own in," Green said.

"That's bull crap," Briggs said. "He ain't one of us."

"I'll do it," Brickhill said. "I'll turn him in and collect the reward."

"Why would you do that?" Green asked. "You're friends."

"We're not friends," Brickhill said. "We just pulled some jobs together over the years."

"Okay, then, that's settled," Briggs said. "We'll snatch 'im and Brick will collect the bounty."

P ALMER WAS DETERMINED to rise early the next morning and make sure that Brickhill and his partners left town. But this evening he had promised to go to Belle Henderson's house for supper with Jeffrey.

He went to his office, found Steve Atlee sitting at the desk.

"Marshal," Atlee greeted him, "I was just gettin' ready to leave."

"You do that, Steve," Palmer said. "I'll be here a while, and then I'm going to Mrs. Henderson's for supper. She's got Jeff there and I have to pick him up."

They changed places, Palmer sitting behind the desk and Atlee standing in front of it.

"But there's something I want to fill you in on before you go," Palmer said.

"What's that, Marshal?"

Palmer told Atlee about the three strangers and how he had "asked" them to leave town the next morning.

"Why did you do that, Marshal?" Atlee asked. "They ain't done nothin'."

"Once I saw them and spoke to them, I knew you were right. They're hard cases, not the type of men we want in this town."

"Are they gonna leave?"

"Tomorrow morning I'll make sure they do," Palmer said.

"I'll meet you here, then," Atlee said. "In case you need me to back you up."

"That's a good idea, Steve," Palmer said. "Meet me here at eight a.m."

"Yes, sir," Atlee said. "I'll be here."

Atlee left and Palmer sat back in his chair and thought about Belle Henderson. He knew the people of Integrity were expecting them to marry, but the two of them had never discussed it. In truth, Palmer would have liked to, but she had already been married to a man who had been living under an assumed name. He didn't want to do that to her again. So he thought if he really wanted to marry her, he had to tell her the truth not only about her husband, but about himself. And then the final decision would be hers.

On the other hand, he could have kept it all a secret from her and married her, anyway. He would just have to hope she never found out the truth.

WHEN IT WAS time to go to Belle's for supper, Palmer left his office and started walking. Along the way he was still wrestling with himself about whether or not to tell her the truth about her husband and about himself and Jeff. Perhaps if he hadn't been so distracted, he would have heard the men coming up behind him as he turned onto Belle's street. He stopped when he felt the gun poke into the small of his back.

"Just take it easy," he heard Rusty Briggs say. "Get his gun. Quick before somebody comes along."

A hand grabbed the gun from his holster, and then a hand took hold of his left arm.

"This way," Briggs said. "And if you resist, I'll shoot you right here."

"What's this all about?" Palmer asked.

"It's about the bounty on a man named Tom Palmer," Briggs said as they pushed Palmer along. "Sound familiar?"

Damn Brickhill, Palmer thought.

"Where were you headed?" Briggs asked him.

"Home," Palmer said.

"Well," Briggs said, "you're not gonna get there."

Palmer saw no point in telling them he was going to Belle's house. Maybe, when he didn't arrive, Belle and Jeff would get worried and start looking for him.

He knew it was Briggs with the gun at his back, but he could also hear the footsteps of two other men behind him, no doubt Brickhill and Chad Green.

"Where are we going?" he asked.

"The stables," Briggs said. "Our horses are saddled and waitin'."

"We goin' on a trip?"

"We are," Briggs said. "We're headin' south, my friend, where turnin' you in is gonna make us pretty rich."

Palmer knew even though he hadn't been in the Southwest for over three-and-a-half years, those wanted posters on him would still be around. He couldn't afford to let the men take him there.

He waited until they got to the livery stables, where four horses—one of which was his gelding—were all saddled and waiting.

"All right," Briggs told him, prodding him with his gun, "get mounted."

Palmer started toward his horse, but turned quickly to bat Briggs' gun hand away. As he did, he saw both Brickhill and Chad Green, and then something hit him on the back of the head and everything went black.

CHAPTER THIRTY-FOUR

"WHERE IS HE?" Belle said aloud.

"He probably got busy," Jeff said. "Three strangers came to town. He's probably watchin' them."

"Then we should eat?"

"Yes."

Belle put supper out on the table and they sat and ate. By the time they finished, they were both worried.

"I'll go home," Jeff said. "Maybe he's there."

"You can stay here, Jeff," she told him.

"It's all right, Belle," he said. He had started out calling her Mrs. Henderson, and then Miss Belle, but eventually she told him to call her Belle. "I'll find 'im."

"Let me know what happened, will you," Belle asked, "when you come to work?"

"I will."

She kissed his cheek and he left. When he got home

and didn't find Palmer there, he went to the office. After that, he went to Steve Atlee's room, which was in the back of a feed store. When Atlee answered, Jeff knew he had awakened the deputy.

"Steve, where's my pa?"

Atlee wiped his face with both hands.

"Last I saw him, he was in the office."

"He's not there, and he's not home."

"Then he's makin' rounds," Atlee said.

"He was supposed to come to Belle's for supper," Jeff said.

"Yeah, he tol' me that."

"He never showed up," Jeff said. "Belle's worried."

Atlee yawned.

"Steve!" Jeff snapped. "I need help findin' my pa."

"Okay, okay," Atlee said. "Let me put on my pants and boots."

He closed the door. Moments later he opened it and stepped out, strapping on his gun.

"We should look in the saloons—" Jeff started.

"No," Atlee said. "He told the three strangers they had to leave town by mornin'. Maybe they didn't like bein' told that."

"What hotel are they in?"

"I don't know, but let's check the livery stable and see if their horses are there."

"And Buddy!" Jeff said. "Pa's horse, too."

"Right. Let's go."

A T THE LIVERY stable they discovered the strangers' three horses were gone, as well as Palmer's.

"Jesus," Jeff said.

"Take it easy," Atlee said. "Maybe he showed them out of town."

"Maybe they took 'im," Jeff said.

"That wouldn't be a smart thing to do, kidnappin' a lawman."

Jeff didn't tell Atlee about Palmer's past, but he was thinking maybe somebody had grabbed him for the price on his head. Palmer had often said his being recognized was a slight possibility. Maybe it had finally happened.

"Don't go overboard, boy," Atlee said. "Let's wait till mornin'—"

"You wait till mornin'," Jeff said. "I'm goin' after them now."

"How?"

"I'll saddle my horse and ride."

"Do you know how to track? How to read sign?"

"Pa showed me some," Jeff admitted.

"And what will you do if they took him and you catch up to them?" Atlee said. "Your pa hasn't taught you how to shoot yet, has he?"

"He ain't," Jeff said, "but he don't know I been practicin' on my own."

"How?" Atlee demanded. "With what gun? You ain't taken any from the office."

"Belle's husband had a gun. I found it one day. I take it out back of her store and practice."

"Rifle or pistol?" Atlee asked.

"Pistol."

"Kid," Atlee said, "you're talkin' about goin' after three hard cases, and you don't know what you're doin'. You could get killed."

"Then come with me and keep me from gettin' killed," Jeff said.

"Jesus," Atlee said, "if somethin' happens to you, your pa'll kill me."

"Not if he's already dead!" Jeff said.

"What makes you think he was taken and didn't go on his own?"

Jeff couldn't answer that question honestly.

"I just have to find him, Steve," Jeff said. "We have to go."

"Well, we can't go in the dark," Atlee said. "So let's give it till mornin' and see if he shows up. If not, then we'll saddle up and go . . . lookin'."

"All right, Steve," Jeff said, "but at first light, I'm goin'."

"You're gonna want to tell Mrs. Henderson you're goin', right?"

Jeff hesitated.

"Well, yeah . . ."

"When?"

"Um, in the mornin'," Jeff said. "She'll be worried, too."

"Then you'll have to wait till she's up," Atlee said. "You're not gonna wanna wake her."

"All right," Jeff said. "She'll be at the store at nine. I'll tell her then."

"Good," Atlee said. "I'll meet you there. Now go home and get some sleep."

"All right," Jeff said, although he didn't think he'd be able to sleep in the empty house. Not when something might have happened to Palmer that he'd been afraid might happen for three-and-a-half years.

Jeff and Deputy Atlee went their separate ways,

supposedly to get some sleep. But while Jeff went home, Atlee walked over to the Palomino Saloon.

W HATAYA MEAN?" WADE the bartender said.
      "Jeff thinks the marshal is missin'," Atlee said. "And he's gonna go lookin' for him."

"Why would Abe be missin'?" Wade asked.

"Jeff won't say," Atlee said, "but it has to do with these three strangers who came to town."

"I haven't heard anythin' about this," Wade said.

"I thought you and Marshal Cassidy were best friends," Atlee explained. "That's why I'm here, to see if you know anything."

"I don't know nothin'," Wade said. "When did these three men get here?"

"Yesterday."

"That's when Abe got back," Wade said. "He hasn't been in to see me yet." Wade frowned. "Makes me think somethin's keepin' him busy."

"And maybe that somethin' now has him missin'," Atlee figured.

"If he wasn't missin', I woulda seen 'im by now," Wade said. "So Jeff might be right. What are you gonna do?"

"Jeff wants to mount up and ride out in the mornin'," Atlee said.

"And go where?"

"That's just it," Atlee said, "if those three have grabbed him and are takin' him somewhere, I don't know where, but Jeff might."

"And he ain't sayin'," Wade said.

"Not to me."

"And he's gonna get himself killed."

"Probably," Deputy Atlee said. "That's why I have to go with him."

"In the mornin'."

"Right," Atlee said, "after he sees Belle Henderson at the store to tell her he's goin'."

"Well, count me in," Wade said. "If you and me let him go after three hard cases alone and he gets killed, we'll never hear the end of it from Marshal Abe Cassidy or Belle Henderson."

"You got that right," Atlee said. "I'm meetin' him at the store at nine."

"I'll be there," Wade said.

"I thought you might wanna be," Atlee said.

"Thanks for lettin' me know," Wade said. "You want a beer while you're here? On the house."

"I won't say no to that," Atlee replied, "but then I'm goin' back to bed."

CHAPTER THIRTY-FIVE

PALMER WOKE TO the bright sun in his eyes and the smell of coffee. He looked around, saw three men by a fire, but when he tried to move, he found he was tied up, hands and feet.

"Hey!" he yelled. "Brick! Goddamn it!"

The three men looked over at him, and Johnny Brickhill came walking over to where Palmer was lying.

"What the hell, Brick?" he said.

"We told you, Tommy," Brickhill said. "We're turnin' you in for the reward. All we gotta do is get you down to New Mexico or Arizona. That's where I remember the biggest price bein' on your head."

"You can't be serious about this, Brick," Palmer said. "I'm a marshal, for Chrissake."

"Only in South Dakota, and only in your county," Brickhill pointed out. "Besides, that's not even your real name."

"How are you going to prove that?" Palmer asked.

"We'll let the law worry about that," Brickhill said. "Now all you have to do is relax."

"How about some coffee?"

"I'll bring you a cup."

"Thanks."

Brickhill went back to the fire, poured a cup of coffee, and started walking back to Palmer.

"What are you doin'?" Rusty Briggs called out.

"I'm givin' Tom some coffee," Brickhill said.

"Then hold the cup for him, because you ain't untyin' him," Briggs said.

"There're three of us here, Rusty," Brickhill said. "He ain't goin' nowhere. I'll untie his hands, but not his feet."

"If he makes a break for it, I'll finish him," Briggs said. "Remember, he's wanted dead or alive."

"You're not going to kill me, Briggs," Palmer called out.

"Why not?"

"Because then you'd have to drag my carcass halfway across the country," Palmer pointed out.

Brickhill laughed.

"He's got a point there, Rusty."

Brickhill untied Palmer's hands and handed him the coffee cup.

"Thanks, Brick. Where the hell are we?"

"A few miles outside of your town," Brickhill said. "We couldn't go too far in the dark, especially not after Chad hit you on the head. After all, we *were* haulin' your carcass."

"I knew I had a headache for some reason," Palmer said, sipping the coffee. He was cold, even though his jacket was buttoned up. The coffee felt good going down. "You know, I'm not going to make this easy for you. I've put too much effort into leaving that life behind me."

"You can leave it behind all you want," Briggs said. "It's still there waitin' for ya."

"And you, or so I hear. What makes you think these two won't turn you in along with me and then split the take two ways?"

"Finish your coffee," Briggs growled, ignoring the question. "We're gonna get movin'. I don't wanna listen to you any longer than I hafta, so you keep talkin' and I'll gag ya the rest of the way."

Palmer drank his coffee, but his mind was working the whole time. . . .

I DON'T LIKE THIS idea, Jeff," Belle said.

"He ain't in town, Belle," Jeff said, "and he wouldn't just leave without tellin' you or me."

"I understand he's missing and somebody has to go looking for him," she said. "I just don't like that it's you."

"Who else is it gonna be?" Jeff asked. "He's my pa."

"Let Deputy Atlee do it," she said. "It's his job."

"If it wasn't for me, he'd still be asleep," Jeff said. "I have to go find him."

"You're not equipped—"

"I lived with the Sioux for six months," he said, cutting her off. "They taught me how to ride. And Pa's taught me some about trackin'."

"What if these three men you're talking about are killers?" Belle asked.

"Me and Steve will handle 'em," Jeff said.

"Do you even know how to shoot?"

"I do," Jeff said. "I been practicin' for . . . a long time."

"And where did you get a gun to practice with?"

"From your back room," Jeff said.

She stared at him for a few tense moments.

"Ken's gun?" she said. "I must have lost track of it after he was killed."

"It was just sittin' there," he argued.

"No," she said, "I forbid it. You can't have it."

"That's okay," Jeff said. "I'll get a gun from the marshal's office."

Belle stared out the front window of her store for a few moments.

"You're determined to do this?" she asked, already knowing the answer.

"Yes!"

And just then Deputy Steve Atlee and another man rode up in front of the store, leading another saddled horse.

"Who's that?" she asked.

Jeff turned and looked.

"That's Wade," he said, surprised, "the bartender from the Palomino. Him and my pa are friends. I guess he's comin', too."

"A deputy, a bartender, and a kid," she said. "Why don't you wait until you can get more men?"

"A posse? In this town?"

"Then I'll come, too," she said suddenly. "I can shoot."

"No!" he said.

"I beg your pardon?"

"If you got hurt, Pa'd never forgive me. We're gonna go find 'im and bring him back."

"Jeff—"

He turned at the door, but the look on his face told her all she needed to know.

"Just . . . be careful."

"I will," he said, and went outside.

"Ready?" Steve Atlee asked.

"Yeah," Jeff said. "Thanks for bringin' me a horse."

He mounted up, then looked over at the bartender, who was holding a shotgun.

"Glad you're comin', Wade," he said.

"I know Abe can take care of himself," Wade said, "but I can't let you go out there and get killed. I'd never hear the end of it from him."

Jeff put his hand on the rifle Steve Atlee had apparently picked out for him.

"I'm ready," he said.

"Good," Atlee said. "Now, where the hell are we goin'?"

"South," Jeff said.

D EADWOOD'S UP AHEAD," Brickhill told Briggs. "Are we stoppin' there?"

"No," Briggs said. "There's no point. We can bypass it and pick up some supplies in a smaller town."

"I ain't never been to Deadwood," Chad Green said. "I'd like to see it."

"When you get your share of the reward money," Briggs said, "come back and do it. But for now forget it. We ain't sightseein'."

"Briggs is right," Brickhill said. "We gotta keep movin' and get this done."

Palmer had the feeling if he could get Brickhill

alone, he could talk him out of turning him in for the reward. The problem was getting him alone.

O KAY, KID," WADE said after they had cleared the town limits, "what's goin' on?"

"What do you mean?"

"I mean," Wade said, "what makes you think your pa's been taken?"

"I know he talked to the three strangers in town," Jeff said.

"That's true," Atlee said. "He told me he ordered them out of town by this mornin'."

"Why'd he do that?" Wade asked.

"Because they looked like trouble."

"I've never known Abe to do that before, no matter how bad a stranger looked. He always gave them a chance. Why were these three different?"

Wade looked at Atlee, who in turn looked at Jeff.

"I don't know," Jeff said. "They just were."

"All right, then," Atlee said, "we're goin' south."

"This snow is days old," Wade said. "Are you gonna be able to pick up some tracks?"

"I hope so."

"I'll be able to recognize the tracks left by Pa's gelding," Jeff told them.

"Oh? Why's that?" Wade asked.

"Pa always told me to look for identifying marks in tracks," Jeff said.

"What's identifying about Abe's geldin'?" Wade asked.

"The size," Jeff said. "Buddy's a big horse."

Wade looked at Atlee.

"He's right," the deputy said. "It's a big horse."

"There are other big horses," Wade said.

"According to the hostler, the strangers' three horses were all normal size."

"You asked?" Atlee said.

"I did before we left," Jeff said.

"That was pretty smart," Wade said.

"I'm not just a dumb kid," Jeff said. "I learned things from the Sioux while I lived with them, and I've learned things these last three years bein' back with . . . with Pa."

"And you're . . . what? Fifteen?" Wade asked.

"Sixteen in a few months."

Wade looked at Atlee.

"So we're gonna let a kid lead us?" the bartender said.

"I guess we are," Deputy Atlee said. "Okay, Jeff, which way?"

CHAPTER THIRTY-SIX

W HEN THEY REACHED the outskirts of a small town called Little River, south of Deadwood, Briggs called for them to camp. Briggs had decided they would cross into Wyoming and then head straight south. The price on Palmer was higher in Arizona and New Mexico, but Briggs wanted to check on it when they reached Colorado. He wanted to get rid of Palmer as soon as possible.

"Chad, build a fire and get some coffee goin'," he said. "Then I want you to ride into town and pick up a few supplies. Johnny, take care of the horses."

"And what do you want me to do, Rusty?" Palmer asked.

"Sit down and shut the hell up!" Briggs snapped.

"I can do that," Palmer said, "as long as I know you're going to feed me when Chad there gets back from town."

"When he gets back, we'll all eat," Briggs said.

He walked Palmer to one side, made him sit with his hands tied behind his back, and then tied his feet.

"Remember," Briggs said, "keep quiet, or you don't eat."

"Got it," Palmer said.

Brickhill finished with the horses, except for Chad Green's, then went to the fire and got the coffee going.

While Palmer watched, Briggs and Brickhill had a conversation at the fire. Then Brickhill brought a cup of coffee over to Palmer and cut his hands loose. Briggs remained by the fire, which gave Palmer a chance.

"Brick," he said, "you can still stop this before we leave the territory."

"Are you wanted in Wyoming?" Brickhill asked. "Is that why you don't wanna leave South Dakota?"

"It doesn't matter where I'm wanted," Palmer said. "You don't want to do this. I know you don't."

"You don't know me, Tom," Brickhill said. "You never did. We just pulled some jobs together."

"You've always been a good man, Brick."

"Horseshit!" Brickhill said. "We're both outlaws and have been for most of our lives. Maybe you tried to change yours, but I haven't."

"I have changed my life, Brick," Palmer said, "and you could, too."

"Not a chance," Brickhill said. "Now drink your coffee and do like Briggs said and keep your mouth shut."

The thing that kept Palmer from talking further was the hunger he felt. He hoped Briggs was being honest about feeding him when Chad Green got back. Once he had something to soothe the hunger pangs, maybe he'd start talking again.

* * *

"WHY HEAD TOWARD Deadwood?" Deputy Atlee asked Jeff.

"Why not?" Jeff asked. "It's the town everybody knows in this territory."

"They could've just headed straight south to Nebraska," Wade said.

Jeff couldn't tell them that Palmer wasn't wanted in Nebraska, so why would anybody take him that way? On the other hand, Palmer himself had told Jeff that though he was definitely wanted in New Mexico, Texas, and Arizona, he wasn't sure about Wyoming and Colorado. But he knew he wasn't wanted in Nebraska or anywhere north of that.

If the three men were taking Palmer in for the reward, they wouldn't be going to Nebraska.

As they approached Deadwood, Jeff reined in his horse and dismounted.

"What is it?" Atlee asked.

Jeff raised a hand to the two men, bidding them wait. He walked around, studying the ground, and then suddenly turned.

"Right here," he said, pointing.

Atlee and Wade both dismounted and walked over to where Jeff was standing.

"See?" Jeff said, still pointing. "That track was left by Pa's geldin'. I'm sure of it."

"It's pretty big, all right," Atlee said. "And there are tracks here for three other horses."

"So where the hell are they takin' him?" Wade asked. "And why?"

Both men looked at the boy.

"I guess we'd just better follow these tracks and find out," Jeff said.

Wade and Atlee looked at each other and shrugged. So far, the boy had apparently been right.

"Then let's mount up and get goin'," Atlee said. "Maybe we can catch them before they leave the territory, and I still have some authority."

Wade didn't bother to point out to Atlee that once they'd left Integrity and the county, he'd already had no standing.

CHAD GREEN RETURNED from Little River with supplies, and before long Brickhill brought Palmer a plate of bacon and beans. Palmer was so hungry, it was as good as a bloody steak.

Briggs, Brickhill, and Chad Green all ate seated around the fire.

"Hey!" Palmer shouted. "It's cold over here. Can't I come by the fire?"

"Shut up!" Briggs shouted back. "Wrap yourself in your blanket."

"Then at least give me another cup of coffee," Palmer said.

"I'll do it," Chad Green said.

He poured a cup and carried it over to Palmer.

"Thanks, kid," Palmer said.

Green squatted in front of Palmer.

"I'm sorry, Marshal," he said. "I'm not in favor of this, but there's nothin' I can do."

"I know, Chad," Palmer said. "I won't hold it against you."

Green stood up and walked back to the fire. Palmer was starting to think maybe it was Green he could use to get out of this, not Brickhill.

He didn't have much hope that anyone from Integrity was coming to help him. The only one there who knew his history was Jeff, and there wasn't much a fifteen-year-old kid could do. Atlee was Palmer's deputy, but why would he suspect that anyone had snatched Palmer to turn him in for a reward?

No, Palmer figured he was on his own if he was going to get out of this. But now that small display of sympathy from the youngest of the three gave him a glimmer of hope that he might escape.

W E HAVE TO stop and camp," Atlee told Jeff. "We can't ride at night."

"I know, I know," Jeff said. "It's just that—"

"We'll catch up to them, Jeff," Wade said. "Now that you've found their trail, they can't get away."

"I just— We just have to get to them while he's still . . . alive," Jeff said. What he really meant was, before they found a place to turn Palmer in.

After Jeff, Atlee, and Wade had camped and built a fire, they supped on beef jerky and coffee since they were light on supplies. All the while Jeff wondered if he was right. Had his "pa" actually been taken by someone who knew him and wanted to collect the reward, or was it something else? What if they were simply taking him someplace to kill him? What if the past of Tom Palmer had nothing to do with this? What if it was all about Marshal Abe Cassidy?

But whichever way this was going, Jeff *had* managed to find their trail, and he had done it quickly enough that they might actually catch up the next day. Then it was just a matter of getting Palmer away from whoever had him.

CHAPTER THIRTY-SEVEN

JEFF WOKE AT first light, wanting to move along, but both Wade and Atlee were in favor of coffee first.

"It's cold, Jeff," Atlee said, "and the tracks ain't goin' anywhere. Let's just have some coffee first, and then we'll go."

Jeff wasn't happy, but he sat at the fire with them and drank the coffee.

"You know," Atlee said, "if Jeff's right about this, I can't help wonderin' what the marshal hasn't told us about himself."

"Whatever he wants to keep private is all right with me," Wade said. "He's my friend—that's all I care about. I wanna get him back alive."

"So do I," Jeff said. "He gave you a badge, Deputy. Why do you have to wonder about anythin'?"

"Whoa, back up, both of you," Atlee said. "I appreciate he gave me a badge. I'm just wonderin' what's goin' on."

"We'll find out when we catch up to them," Jeff said. "Now can we go?"

Wade dumped the remnants of the coffeepot onto the fire and stood up.

"All right. Let's move."

W HEN THEY ENTERED Wyoming, crossing the border north of Rapid City, South Dakota, Briggs reined in, stopping the others behind him.

"Okay, listen," he said. "I can't go into town with you. I know I'm wanted hereabouts, but we need to find out if Palmer is. The only way to do that is to go to the law and ask. You two have to do that."

"Talk to the law?" Chad Green asked.

"Why don't you keep Chad here, Rusty?" Brickhill said. "I'll go in and find out. But I think we're gonna hafta go farther south."

"There ain't no harm in askin'," Briggs said. "Casper is that way. I've been there, and they have a sheriff's office. Just make like you're a bounty hunter. Ask if he's heard of Palmer and if you can look at his posters."

"I'll get it done," Brickhill said. He looked at Palmer. "You wanna tell us if you're wanted in Wyomin' and save me the trip?"

"Sorry," Palmer said. "It's been a while and I can't remember."

"Yeah, right," Briggs said. "I know every reward that's out on me."

"You have a better memory than me, then."

"Brick, we're gonna continue to ride south. You'll have to catch up with us with whatever you find out. We'll be headin' for Laramie."

"Got it," Brickhill said. "I'll be seein' you both."

He turned his horse and rode off toward Casper.

"Chad," Briggs said, "I want you to ride behind Palmer. If he tries to make a break for it, we shoot 'im. Got that?"

"Yeah, Rusty," Green said, "I got it."

Palmer had thought that Brickhill would be his best way out, but now he was thinking he might get away while the man was in Casper. He was pretty sure the youngster Chad would hesitate before he fired. But there was no telling how much time he would have to make it happen.

T HEY'RE NOT GOIN' to Deadwood," Atlee said. "They veered off here."

"Headin' for Rapid City?" Wade wondered aloud.

"Or Wyoming," Jeff said.

"Only one way to find out," the deputy said. "As long as we have these big gelding's tracks to follow."

"How fresh are these?" Wade asked. "Can you tell?"

"Not really," Atlee said. "It's just not what I'm good at." He looked over at the young man. "Jeff? Can you tell?"

"From what my pa's taught me," Jeff said, "I'd say at least half a day."

"Well," Wade said, "they did have almost a day's head start, but they had to camp overnight like we did."

"We didn't find a campfire," Atlee pointed out.

"That doesn't mean they didn't make one," Wade said. "We just didn't come across it. Let's keep on movin' and see where we end up."

"Agreed," Atlee said. "Let's keep movin'."

THE SHERIFF OF Casper had never heard of Tom Palmer.

"What makes you think he's wanted in Wyoming?" Sheriff Holliday asked Johnny Brickhill.

"I don't think he is," Brickhill said, "I was just checking."

"Why?" the lawman asked. "Is he in the area?"

"I heard somethin' about him while I was in Deadwood. He wasn't wanted there, so I thought when I crossed the border, I'd check."

"Well, you're welcome to look at my posters," the sheriff said.

"I don't think I need to do that, Sheriff," Brickhill said. "Thanks for your time."

He left the office and mounted his horse. He didn't want to spend any more time in the lawman's office than he had to, and looking at posters would have been tedious. So he just headed out of town, riding hard to catch up with the others. He was pretty sure they would end up turning Palmer over to the law in either New Mexico or Texas.

THEY SPLIT UP here," Atlee said. "I may not be an expert tracker, but I can see that."

"He's right," Jeff said, pointing. "One went that way, and the other three kept goin' south."

"And the marshal's geldin'?" Wade asked.

"South," Atlee said.

"So then I guess we keep goin' south," the bartender said.

"Why would one of them split off from the others?" Jeff asked.

"There's a town called Casper that way," Atlee said. "Maybe they sent one man for supplies."

"Sounds right to me," Wade said. "We still have a few hours of daylight. Let's not waste them."

"Right," Atlee said, and they headed south.

PALMER CONSIDERED TRYING to ride away from Briggs and Chad Green with his hands tied behind his back, but he knew he'd end up falling off the gelding. He was going to have to make a move while his hands were untied, and that was only when they were camped and ready to eat.

He knew they wouldn't get to Laramie before dark, so they were going to have to make camp. If Brickhill didn't catch up, Palmer would have to get away from only Briggs and Green, either while they were eating their supper or breakfast.

"We're gonna camp here," Briggs called out. "Chad, get him off his horse and tied down."

"Right."

Briggs turned in his saddle before dismounting and looked behind them. He didn't see any sign of Brickhill.

"He'll catch up, Rusty," Green said, helping Palmer off his horse.

"Yeah, he will," Briggs said.

* * *

IT WAS STARTING to get dark when Brickhill caught the scent of coffee. He moved cautiously, as he figured the others would have been much farther ahead of him than this. When he spotted the campfire, he assumed it wasn't them.

He dismounted and tied his horse to a tree, then began to move on foot toward the camp. It was now dark, and his intention had been to continue to ride despite that, taking all precautions. He would have stopped eventually to camp, but he wanted to get a few more miles under him so that he would be sure to catch up to the others the next afternoon.

But now he crept forward, keeping as quiet as possible. If he saw Briggs and Chad Green at the fire, then it would be clear something had happened to slow them down. At that time he'd fetch his horse and join them. But if there were strangers in camp, he was going to watch and listen before deciding to reveal himself. Maybe they'd have some bacon and invite him to eat with them.

When he came within sight of the camp, he crouched behind some bushes and watched. He saw three men, but not the three he was looking for.

He decided to get closer so he could hear their conversation. . . .

ATLEE, WADE, AND Jeff were sitting around the fire, drinking coffee. They still had only beef jerky to eat.

"If we're gonna keep at this," the deputy said, "we're gonna need supplies."

"We can stop at the next town," Wade said. "We won't need much. We can't weight ourselves down if we're gonna catch up to them."

"I still wish we knew who we were catching up with and why," Atlee said.

"You're doin' your job, Deputy," Wade said. "You should be happy with that."

Atlee looked at Jeff, saw that the boy was looking into the fire.

"I'll bet your pa told you not to do that," he said.

"Do what?" Jeff asked.

"Stare into the fire," Atlee said. "You're ruinin' your night vision."

"Oh, yeah . . ." Jeff said. "Sorry. Are we gonna stand watch?"

"Probably a good idea," Atlee said. "I'll go first, then wake Wade, and then he'll wake you. Now get some sleep. Hopefully, we'll catch up to your pa tomorrow."

"Fine."

Jeff rolled himself up in his blanket and fell asleep.

CHAPTER THIRTY-EIGHT

B RICKHILL CAUGHT UP to Briggs, Green, and the marshal at noon the next day.

Briggs heard the horse behind them and reined in to turn and look.

"It's Brick," Chad Green called out.

With Brickhill out of the camp, Briggs had left Palmer's hands tied when he woke up. Palmer had never had a chance to make a move.

"What'd you find out?" Briggs asked when Brickhill caught up.

"Nothin' in Casper," Brickhill said, "but I found out some things on the way back."

"Like what?"

"Like there are three men tracking us," Brickhill said. "A deputy, a kid, and one other man."

"A posse?" Briggs said. "Why?"

"Not a posse," Brickhill said. "Apparently, the kid is Palmer's."

"He has a son?"

"That's what it looks like," Brickhill said. "And they're gonna try to get him back. I had to ride all night to make sure I got here with enough time. I'm gonna say they're about six hours behind us."

"Okay," Briggs said, "that gives us time to come up with a plan."

"Why don't we just outrun 'em?" Chad Green asked.

"We probably could if we weren't draggin' him along," Briggs said, indicating Palmer.

"Then maybe this wasn't such a good idea," Brickhill said.

"No," Briggs said, "it's easy money. All we gotta do is get rid of this deputy and whoever's ridin' with him."

"And the kid," Green said.

Briggs looked at him.

"Maybe I'll leave the kid to you, Chad," he said. "You should be able to handle 'im."

"Whataya wanna do, Rusty?" Brickhill asked.

"Let's keep ridin' until we find a likely spot for an ambush," Briggs said. "Once we take care of 'em, we only gotta collect the reward."

Listening to them plan an ambush of Jeff, Steve Atlee, and a third man Palmer could only assume was Wade, he strained against his ropes to no avail. He had to find some way to get loose, or else he'd have to watch Jeff and the others be killed—and all because of his outlaw past.

* * *

JEFF WOKE ATLEE and Wade the next morning and they all had some coffee to warm themselves before they started out.

"How was everythin' last night?" Atlee asked Jeff.

"Well," Jeff said, "I didn't see anythin', but . . ."

"But what?" Atlee asked.

"I just had a funny feelin', like somebody was out there . . . watchin' us."

Atlee looked at Wade.

"How about you?"

"Now that you mention it," Wade said, "I did get that feelin' last night, but not durin' my watch."

"The same with me," Jeff said. "It was last night, not early this mornin'."

"Well," Atlee said, "we could go and have a look through the brush, see if there's any indication that someone was there watchin' us."

"Then we'll lose the ground we've been makin' up on them, won't we?" Jeff asked.

"The boy's right," Wade said. "We should keep movin'."

"Okay," Atlee said, "but if they sent somebody to watch their back trail and he spotted us, then they know we're comin'. We'll have to be extra careful the rest of the way."

"It's odd . . ." Jeff said.

"What is?" Atlee asked.

"How sometimes you can just feel when somebody is watchin' you."

"Your pa would say you had good instincts, Jeff," Wade said. "And at this point, I'd say I'd agree with him."

A BOUT TEN MILES outside of Laramie, Rusty Briggs held up his hand.

"Here," he said. "This is a good place for an ambush. We can wait on either side for them to come around this bend."

Palmer looked around. There was plenty of cover, rocks and trees, for Briggs and his men to make an effective ambush.

"You don't have to kill them," Palmer said.

The three outlaws looked at him.

"Then how would you suggest we get them off our trail?" Briggs asked.

"That's easy," Palmer said. "Let me talk to them."

"And tell them what?"

"I'll tell them that I came with you willingly. That there's no sense in them following us any farther."

"And I suppose they'd believe that, huh?" Brickhill asked.

"I'll make them believe it," Palmer said.

"And we're supposed to believe you'd do that," Briggs said. "Why?"

"Because I don't want to be the reason they're all killed," Palmer explained.

"And the boy with them," Johnny Brickhill said. "Is he your son?"

"It's . . . complicated," Palmer said. "He was rescued from the Sioux, and I sort of . . . adopted him."

"And one's your deputy," Brickhill said. "Who's the third man?"

"I can't know for sure," Palmer answered, "but I'd guess it's a friend of mine named Wade. He's a bartender at the Palomino Saloon."

Briggs looked at Brickhill and Green.

"One deputy with a bartender and a boy," he said, a wolfish grin on his face. "They're gonna be real easy pickin's."

"Now wait—"

"You'll be trussed up and gagged," Briggs told him, cutting him off, "and set up so you can watch the whole thing." He looked at his men. "If they're six hours behind us, they'll still be here while it's light. Let's get set up."

L OOKS LIKE THEY'RE headin' for Laramie," Steve Atlee said, pointing ahead.

"If we could get to a town with a telegraph," Wade said, "we could send word ahead to the law there."

"The only problem is," Atlee said, "we still don't know for sure that the marshal is bein' held against his will."

"He is!" Jeff said.

"The deputy's right, Jeff," Wade said. "We can't tell the law in Laramie that, for sure."

"Plus finding a town with a telegraph would delay us and put them farther ahead. What if we sent a telegram to Laramie after they were already there and gone?"

"So we just keep goin'?" Wade asked.

"Yes!" Jeff said.

Both Atlee and Wade smiled at the sound of the boy's relief.

B RIGGS TIED PALMER firmly to a tree and gagged him, then Briggs and Green took up positions on both sides of the road. Briggs then sent Brickhill back a mile to keep watch.

CHAPTER THIRTY-NINE

B RICKHILL SPOTTED THE three men approaching and rode at a gallop back to the ambush point.

"They're comin'," he told Briggs.

"It's about time," Briggs said. "It's gonna be dark in an hour. Let's get this done!"

Palmer's frustration was mounting. His heart was racing and he was sweating despite the cold. Rusty Briggs himself had tied Palmer up and had three times come over to check and make sure he was still secure.

Palmer had no choice but to sit there and watch the whole thing unfold.

W AIT," JEFF CALLED out.
       Atlee and Wade both reined in and turned to look at the boy, who was studying the ground.

"What is it?"

"There are tracks here that've been left recently."

"How recent?" Atlee asked.

"Less than an hour, I'd say," Jeff answered.

"How can you tell?" Wade asked.

"Fresh tracks are fresh tracks, Wade," Jeff said. "My pa would say a breeze hasn't even disturbed these yet."

"These could've been left by the same man we think was watchin' us in camp," Atlee said. "If he's ridin' just ahead of us, then he can warn them that we're comin'."

"Warn who?" Wade asked.

"That's the question," Atlee said. "All we know is it could be those three strangers from town."

"Unless it was somebody else who took the marshal," Wade said.

"If he was taken," Atlee said.

"Don't start that again," Jeff said. "He was taken, and he's just ahead of us with whoever took 'im."

"Right," Atlee said.

"So if they're waitin' for us," Wade said, "what do we do?"

"Simple," Atlee said. "We make them keep waitin'."

I T WAS STARTING to get dark and Rusty Briggs was getting impatient. He had Brickhill stationed on the same side of the road as him and Chad Green on the other side. Now he left his position and went over to where Brickhill was crouched.

"So where are they?" he asked.

"They shoulda been here by now."

"Well, get to higher ground and take a look," Briggs said. "Chad and me, we'll stay in place."

"I could run smack into them—"

"If you do," Briggs said, "you better start shootin'."

Briggs turned to go back to his position. Brickhill started off on foot, seeking higher ground from where he could get a good look behind them.

A TLEE AND WADE were riding slowly, now following the fresh trail rather than the older one.

"You think we did the right thing with the kid?" Wade asked.

"He did live with the Sioux for six months," Atlee said. "He learned some things."

"Whoa," Wade said, looking ahead.

"What is it?"

"I thought I saw someone," the bartender said.

"Where?"

"On that bluff," Wade said, pointing with his chin. "It was quick, but . . ."

They both stared ahead, saw nothing.

"Let's go easy, Wade," Atlee said. "We may be gettin' closer."

"Yeah, but why?" Wade asked.

"What?"

"Why are we gettin' closer?" Wade said. "We're ridin' slower, so . . ."

"So they may be waitin' for us."

Wade nodded.

"I hope the kid's gonna be okay," he said.

B RICKHILL CAME RUNNING back to Briggs.
"They're comin'," he said.

Briggs turned and looked at the trussed-up Palmer.

"Hear that?" Briggs said. "Make sure you watch closely."

Palmer struggled, but he was tied tight.

"Get back in place," Briggs told Brickhill.

"Right."

"And don't fire until I do."

Brickhill heard him, but Chad Green didn't.

B OTH WADE AND Atlee kept their eyes on the bluff, but never saw anyone. They kept their eyes on it anyway as they passed, and then followed the bend in the road. . . .

C HAD GREEN SAW the riders coming around the bend, aimed his rifle, and fired.

Across the way Briggs shouted, "Damn it!" as he wanted to let them get closer. Now he had no choice. He stood up, aimed, and fired as he stepped out from cover.

Briggs heard the two shots, saw one of the riders get knocked from his saddle.

C HAD GREEN'S BULLET hit Wade in the shoulder, knocking him from his horse. The animal reared, came down, and struck the bartender in the head. The metal horseshoe crushed the man's skull.

The second shot whizzed past Atlee as he looked to see where the shots were coming from. He saw the three men stepping from cover, their rifles coming to bear on him. . . .

* * *

PALMER SAW WADE fall from his horse, watched as Deputy Atlee froze in his saddle. Then he felt something behind him.

"I'm here, Pa," Jeff said. "I'll cut you loose."

The boy used his knife to cut the ropes, then removed the gag.

"Do you have a gun?" Palmer asked.

Jeff handed Palmer a rifle, then showed him the pistol in his other hand.

"All right, boy," Palmer said. "Let's go."

Palmer's legs failed him the first time he tried to get up, so Jeff helped him to his feet. They both looked in the direction the shots were coming from.

Palmer had taken his eyes off of Atlee, so he didn't see the deputy leap from his saddle to the ground as the three outlaws began to fire at him. At least one bullet struck his horse, and the animal crumpled to the ground.

As Palmer watched, Atlee scrambled across the ground and took cover behind the fallen horse.

The three outlaws began to advance on him, still unaware that Palmer was loose.

Atlee fired several times, and Chad Green spun on his heels as one bullet struck him.

"Briggs!" Palmer shouted.

As Briggs turned to look at him, both Palmer and Jeff fired their weapons. Both their bullets struck Briggs in the chest, knocking him back on his heels and then down onto his back.

Brickhill turned to see who had shot Briggs, saw Palmer and the boy advancing on him. He then looked behind him, saw the deputy rise and start walking toward him in the dying light.

"It's over, Brick," Palmer called out.

"This wasn't my idea, Tom," Brickhill said, his gun still in his hand.

"Just drop the gun," Palmer commanded.

"I can't," Brickhill said. He looked back at the deputy again. "Why don't you just let me go, and your deputy doesn't have to hear any of your history? Whataya say?"

Palmer raised his rifle. Brickhill looked shocked, started to raise his pistol, but Palmer shot him in the chest before he could bring it to bear.

Atlee checked the bodies of Briggs and Chad Green, saw they were dead, and continued on to where Brickhill was lying.

"They're all dead," he said as he reached Palmer and Jeff.

"And Wade?" Palmer asked.

"Also dead," Atlee said. "Sorry, Marshal."

Palmer looked at Jeff standing alongside him and then put his arm around the boy.

"Where'd you learn to shoot like that?" he asked.

"I've been practicin'," Jeff said.

"We're going to talk about that," Palmer told him.

CHAPTER FORTY

PALMER SAT AT his desk and stared. He still wasn't sure he hadn't murdered Johnny Brickhill just to keep him from telling Steve Atlee who he really was. He replayed the events that had taken place several days before, still unsure who had raised their gun first, him or Brickhill.

When they got back to Integrity—having buried all the dead before heading back, including Wade—Palmer had waited till he and Atlee were alone in the office.

"Why the hell did you bring Jeff out there?" he demanded.

"Marshal, it was the kid who figured out that you got took and hadn't left on your own," Atlee said.

"Why the hell would I leave on my own?"

"I don't know, Marshal," Atlee said. "I didn't know

that or why anybody would take you. But Wade and me, we were convinced by Jeff to follow you. The boy was real persuasive."

"So you tracked us?" Palmer asked.

"Actually, Jeff did most of the sign readin'," Atlee said. "He's pretty good."

"I tried to teach him what I know," Palmer said. "I guess he put that together with what he learned from the Sioux."

"Marshal, can I ask you . . . why did they kidnap you? Where were they takin' you?"

Palmer had been waiting for that question.

"I still don't know, Deputy," he said. "I couldn't get them to tell me anything once they dragged me out of town."

"Did you know any of them?" Atlee asked.

Palmer still didn't know if Atlee had heard anything Brickhill had said to him before he shot him, but he took a chance, anyway.

"No," he said, "I never saw any of them before in my life."

ATLEE HAD NOT questioned Palmer about it again. So the only thing niggling at Palmer was, had he had to kill Brickhill? Had he done it just to keep the man quiet? If he had, that was certainly not the action of the lawman he thought he was, but rather the outlaw he once was.

The only other fallout he had to deal with from the experience was twofold. First, he had to deal with the fact that Jeff wasn't a kid anymore. Not after he had tracked Palmer and the outlaws all that way and ended up shooting one of them.

Atlee and Wade had allowed Jeff to veer off from them, off the main road, in an attempt to locate Palmer and his captors. When Jeff had heard the shots, he hurried toward them and found Palmer tied to the tree. He untied him, gave him the rifle he'd been given from the office gun rack, and drew Belle's husband's pistol from his belt. The boy fired one shot from that gun with deadly accuracy. Palmer still had to deal with the fact that the boy had been practicing behind his back.

Second, there was Belle. Could he ask her to marry him, knowing it would be the second time she married a man without knowing his true identity? Or could he reveal the true identities of her husband and himself to her and expect anything good to come of it?

Palmer had allowed a couple of days to go by without confronting his issues with Jeff and Belle. He was hoping for some kind of inspiration on how to handle everything, but nothing was coming.

Johnny Brickhill coming to Integrity and recognizing him was his worst nightmare. Could it happen again? Probably. Maybe he should take Jeff and just move, go farther north, make his outlaw days a more distant past—only would they be?

And maybe what he truly needed was to talk to someone about all this, say it out loud so he could hear it. At one time that would have been Wade, but he had lost his best friend. His past had gotten the bartender killed. And his past could come back again.

There were only two people in town he could talk to about any of this, and it was time to do it.

* * *

H E WENT HOME and found Jeff sitting on the front porch of the house he was supposed to have been sharing with his parents and brothers and sisters. Palmer mounted the front porch and sat next to the boy.

"I'm sorry," he said.

"For what?"

"For everything I've put you through."

Jeff looked at Palmer and said, "You gave me a life."

"And you saved mine," Palmer said.

"So we ain't got nothin' to be sorry for," Jeff said, and then added, "Pa." He would call Palmer that in front of other people, but usually not when they were alone.

"Well, you don't," Palmer said. "I've got a whole past to be sorry for."

"But you gave up that life," Jeff said.

"I might have, but it came back and got Wade killed. Not to mention three other men."

"That wasn't your fault," Jeff said. "Pa, we got a good life here."

"As long as nobody else from my past comes along to mess it up," Palmer said.

"Well, you know," Jeff said, "keep shavin'."

That was true. Had Palmer been clean-shaven and had a haircut, Brickhill might not have even noticed him, and the three men might have moved on.

"You know, there's still something else we have to talk about."

"What's that?"

"You and that gun you've been practicing with."

"Aw, Pa," Jeff said, "I just wanted to—"

"We're going to have to get you a better gun," Palmer went on.

Jeff brightened.

"Really?" he said.

"I'm sorry you had to kill a man at fifteen, Jeff," Palmer said, "although I think it was my bullet that killed him."

"Aw, Pa—"

"Come on," Palmer said. "I promised Belle we'd be at her house for supper."

They stood up and started walking.

"When are you gonna ask 'er to marry ya, Pa?"

"You want me to do that?"

"Well, sure," Jeff said. "Havin' her cook all our meals would be the only way our life here could be even better."

Palmer cuffed the boy behind the head playfully.

"There's a problem with that, Jeff."

"What's that?"

"How can I marry her when she wouldn't know who she's really marrying?"

"She knows who you are now," Jeff said. "Ain't that all that matters?"

"I don't know," Palmer said. "I've been struggling with that question."

"What do you think would happen if you told 'er?" Jeff asked.

"I'm afraid she wouldn't want anything to do with me," Palmer said.

"Seems to me she likes the man you are now," Jeff

said. "Maybe she wouldn't care about the man you once was. But what do I know?·I'm just a kid."

"And when did you get to be such a smart kid?" Palmer asked.

SUPPER WAS A happy affair, because Palmer and Jeff were back in Integrity, safe and sound. It was the first time since their return that Belle and the men were all together celebrating that fact.

When Belle went back to the stove to load up their bowls with seconds, Jeff leaned over and asked, "When are you gonna ask 'er?"

"Well, I'm not going to do it with you sitting here," Palmer said.

"I ain't done eatin' yet," Jeff said. "When I am, I'll go out on the porch."

"What are you two whisperin' about?" Belle asked as she returned to the table.

"Nothing," Palmer said.

"Just man talk," Jeff said.

"Oh, is that right?" Belle asked. She reached over and grabbed Jeff's ear. "So you're a man now?"

"He sure is," Palmer said, but he didn't go any further. They hadn't told Belle everything that had happened on the trail, so she had no idea that Jeff had shot a man.

"Well," she said, releasing his ear, "after he went out there and found you and brought you back, I guess he is."

After they finished their second helpings, Jeff stood up and said, "I'm gonna go sit out front and . . . whittle."

"Make sure you come back in for dessert," Belle

told him. She looked at Palmer. "When did that boy start to whittle?"

"He's not whittling," Palmer said. "He's just leaving us alone for a little while."

"Oh? Why's he doin' that?"

Palmer studied Belle Henderson. She had been working all day and then all evening in the kitchen. She was wearing a simple cotton dress with an apron over it. A few locks of hair had come loose from behind her head and they were hanging down over her eyes. And to Palmer, she looked radiant.

She was taking dishes from the table to the sink, so he said, "Sit for a few minutes, Belle. We need to talk."

"Uh-oh," she said, "this sounds serious." She sat across from him, folded her hands on the table, and stared. "What is it?"

"I guess you know folks in town are expecting us to get married."

"Really?" she asked. "Is that what they're expectin'? Because I haven't even been asked yet."

"I want to ask you," he said, "but there are some things you should know first."

"I think I know all I need to know, Abe," she said.

"My name," he said, almost choking on the words, "it's not really Abe—"

"Stop," she said, holding one hand up. "If you're gonna tell me that you changed your name to get away from your checkered past, I've been through that already. My first husband wasn't named Henderson."

"You knew that?" he asked.

"Of course I knew it," she said. "He told me before we married, and I accepted him."

"No matter how bad his past was?" Palmer asked.

"He was tryin' to get away from that past and start again," Belle said. "I think everybody's got a right to do that, don't you?"

"That was what I hoped," he said.

"So if you're gettin' ready to tell me what a bad man you once were, don't. If you're gonna ask me to marry you, I'm only gonna consider the man you are now when I give you my answer. So . . . are you gonna ask?"

He reached across the table, took her hand, and asked, "Belle, will you marry me?"

"Of course I will, you silly man," she said. "Isn't that what the town expects?"

Ready to find
your next great read?

Let us help.

Visit prh.com/nextread

Penguin
Random
House